Ways to Read
The World

Stories in Triptych

Ways to Read
The World

Stories in Triptych

Robert Scotellaro

ISBN: 979-8-9858479-0-1

https://scanticbooks.blogspot.com
Facebook: Scantic Books

for Diana and Katie

Also by Robert Scotellaro

Fiction

What Are the Chances?
Nothing Is Ever One Thing
Bad Motel
What We Know So Far
Measuring the Distance

Anthology

New Micro: *Exceptionally Short Fiction*
(Co-edited with James Thomas)

Poetry

After the Revolution
The Night Sings A Capella
Rhapsody of Fallen Objects
My Father's Cadillac
Early Love Poems of Genghis Khan
Blinded by Halos
East Harlem Poems

For Children

Snail Stampede
Dancing with Frankenstein
Carla and the Greedy Merchant
The Terrible Storm

Table of Contents

"The truth is rarely pure, and never simple."

Oscar Wilde

Niagara Falls

High-Stakes

Picture a man of average stature and looks seated beside a woman of average stature and looks on a flight to New York from small Midwestern towns. Picture him telling her he is a high-stakes mogul on his way to put a bow on a deal involving an entire block of buildings, what he'd like her to imagine as skyscrapers. Picture him dressed, not as a real estate magnate, but more a poor pig farmer on his way to church.

Imagine him opening the small bag of peanuts, delicately, as if he's unlocking the secrets in an ancient scroll. See her looking out the window down at shapes of land sculptured by distance into manageable puzzle pieces, saying: "It's so beautiful." Wisps of clouds pass and grow denser as he leans over her to look also and a single peanut lands on her lap, on her dress. On a print of an elegant flower ever so slightly faded. Only a bit out of season.

"Wow," he says, "cool." And the word *cool* flaps around for a moment like a fish on a rock. Picture her watch, with an askance glance, as the peanut rolls to the floor.

Broken Ice

Picture an inexpensive hotel in the city with an ice machine in the hall that no longer works properly. Picture them after. After a misshapen moment when he fumbles with a condom, puts it on backwards. Imagine what was empty space between them remaining so. Picture a TV on, a bit past the foot of the bed—an overzealous commercial announcer's voice like a madman's mantra they hardly hear, as she tells him she was once the Iowa State Ice Skating Champion. "Gosh," she says, "the trophy was so big you needed body builders to lift it." Even though she ice skated only once in her life, on a frozen lake her brother fell in. The sound of the ice cracking at first like cubes in a cold drink by a microphone, then thunderous as he crashed through. Some men forming a linked line, lying on their bellies to retrieve him. How that was the first and last time she wore skates. Picture how easily the words leave her lips. Spill out like a falls, not Niagara. But *her* Niagara.

Picture him saying "Wow" (without the "Cool" this time) looking at her teeth. Imagine him thinking how a retainer, when she was young, would have spared her that overbite.

Spring-Loaded

Picture them going to Coney Island the next day. Digging their feet into the sand, listening to the monosyllabic sea shanties the gulls are singing. Picture them watching the tide come in, go out, with their belladonna eyes sea-absent Midwesterners possess when confronted with such wet, wavy vastness. He has a *dental appliances* convention to attend early the next day and his mind is meandering as a small cyclone might. He needs to call his wife, imagines telling her of the wondrous new materials they've come up with for night guards. Picture the woman beside him digging those skate-phobic feet further into the sand to the cool spaces where the sand darkens.

Imagine her thinking of her husband back home with the kids. Thinking of the dull neckties he wears: mulch brown and dull end-of-autumn greens. Always on crooked. How she straightens them on the way to church. How they always go back, as if spring-loaded, crooked. How she can't wait to see that Broadway play with her younger sister who moved to this hulking town. Imagine her thinking how badly the man beside her smells. Never taking a shower afterwards. Imagine her recalling how he looked up at those skyscrapers (reverentially) as if they were holy/poking halfway into Heaven. *Some magnate!*

Imagine him turning and hoping she'll smile so he can see her teeth again. Picture her gazing at his open shirt, at his undershirt on backwards and inside out, at that little twisted label. Imagine the silence between them like a tightrope, slack and greased. Picture the gulls overhead getting every word right, the tide getting every word right.

The Pizza Man

Attic Status

The pizza delivery man knows he has bigger fish to fry in this world. He knows it in his bones. Feels it like a xylophone being played against his ribcage: clear resonating notes.

The top half of his military dress uniform is on his mother's mannequin torso (with all his medals attached) along with his spelling bee trophies in the attic.

He rings each doorbell with precision (that trigger finger repurposed) and like a jack-in-the-box, a happy face springs up every time.

Checklists

Highpoints: he'd once won a cow patty flinging contest, made love to his wrestling coach's hot young wife, guessed the right phrases on *Wheel of Fortune* fourteen times in a row …

To do: organize a few of his army airborne buddies to form a skydiving group called, The Skydiving Draculas (akin to the

Flying Elvises) only they'd have fangs and wouldn't wear anything with glitter, but there'd be capes in both cases, get Shelia a *real* diamond ring (regardless of how big) instead of the fake one she currently has, become a pet therapist (he knows he'd be a natural), learn a dead language (preferably Latin) so that he can one day call upon it in proper company: that singularly wise and apt phrase at his fingertips in lieu of the pizza delivery tips at his fingertips.

Satin Latin

He and Shelia lived in a car for a time, and now they have a small, clean apartment they take pride in renting. There's a job interview he's going to the next day and he lays out two neckties he's gotten from the thrift store.

"Which one?" he asks.

"I think blue suits you," Sheila says, and a whiff of something, most likely inapplicable, passes through him. A metaphor? Double entendre? Some way she perceives him: blue? He hisses open a can of beer, puts his arm around her on the couch. They are waiting for a favorite comedy show. She asks if he's had a good day. Made a lot of tips? He doesn't respond. Turns up the volume and mumbles under his breath: *aqula non capit* (the eagle does not catch flies).

"What?" she says.

"Gibberish," he says, hugging her closer, then notices her cat keeps looking over at him between faux flea scratching (or what he deems as such). Decides he is too tired to pull back the curtain. Looks straight ahead instead. Soon enough, the TV light and bursts of canned laughter will be more than enough to settle everything.

Disneyland on Mars

Colorfast

Loraine dyes hair out of her kitchen on weekends. Gets all the choicest gossip. Has a knack for matching tones, colorfast. Has a knack for loosening tongues. During the week she waits tables at *The Blue Plate Diner,* where she also has a knack for selectively swishing her hips. But keeps it measured. Doesn't go hula dancing around with a plate of pancakes, but knows how to shift her weight, just so, for the big tippers.

Now it's, "Oh dearie, you know he'd go hog-wild with half a whiff of encouragement." Then she proceeds to take years off all that gray. Wishes she could be pampered like that with praise and privilege. But, "Money doesn't grow on trees," she's fond of saying, "leaves do."

Spitting

Floyd is out back with a friend. They sit in beach chairs, spitting. Taking turns. Floyd tried to explain once how guys like to spit sometimes to accent one point or other. Or just express a certain emotion better than words alone can. A quick, light spritz from between your teeth could mean: "Oh, well ..." Or: "Hell, that's life ..." A far flung throat-clearing high velocity wad could mean there was a broken heart involved, or revenge rising up and torpedoing out. How there were many styles and nuances between.

Loraine thinks it's crude. Wants to talk to him like she might their six-year-old: "Use your words. That's what they're for. Spit's for swallowing. Ain't you heard?"

Life Among the Mole People

Loraine is a great dancer. She wants to drag Floyd out from that damn man cave in the basement. The game is on and his beer bottle is near and dear. She wants the two of them to dress up fancy and go ballroom dancing. Floyd tells her he's got two left feet and can't change that. God made him that way. Then he sticks his head back inside the TV and starts running down the field side-by-side with some behemoth or other, screaming out when they both make it into the end zone. Loraine wishes she could say, "Well, damn!" and spit a long bullet of saliva across the room.

When Loraine was younger, she wanted to be a Disney character in one of those plush cartoon suits, a chipmunk, say (it didn't matter what/which) greeting kids at Disneyland. Imagined herself waving, giving them hugs, thought how great it would be to be somebody/something else. Look out without anybody looking in. But she never did make it out of Harlan County. Even with all that electric hope charged up inside her. She just ran/danced in place most times, till she was too exhausted to make any more of it. Another knack she had.

The Widower's Feathers

Spinal Stanzas

He has Emily Dickinson poems tattooed across the near sum
of him. In Times New Roman as if they were typed there. This
is the part of him known only to the women he dates. Privy to
the shock of them excavated in dim light as he disrobes.

After, through a lacquer of sweat, he asks the most in-
trigued of them to read the ones on his back he cannot see.
Who contemplate their meaning, tangled in an enigma of syntax and turns of phrase. A nurse once saying, "I like the one
by your L5 vertebra," squinting up close to it, her glasses on
his nightstand.

Hubba-Hubba

He had a wife, a poet, to share this ranch with. She is gone,
but the peacocks remain. They are everywhere on the property, their shrill cries belying the elegance of their feathery
sprays fanned out to infinity. The cocks showing off their

hubba-hubba plumes. He likes to think of himself, in a more erudite fashion, similarly. But the women he meets, unlike his wife, are used to inked hula dancers, devils with pitchforks, and interlocking Celtic patterns. But are nonetheless taken at the sight of him. A book they'd never read under different circumstances, marginally pondered over before a joint is lit, a beer cracked open.

Through the Chill Light

Still, he feels her out there, through the whiskey vapors, the chill light of dating sites frosting his computer screen. The one who'll stitch a gaze to every word, puzzle them/him out. Never fully knowing, but wanting to. *Breath and shadow.* Asking him to turn over and over like pages.

From a Hitman's Sketchy Last Will and Testament Written on a Placemat at The House of Pancakes

P.S.

You'll find the key to a safety deposit box in the hollowed out copy of the one Agatha Christie novel in my bookcase. Sorry I cannot disclose how I came upon all that cash but since you are an only child IT'S ALL YOURS. Let's just say it came from "investments" and leave it at that. Too bad your ma isn't still alive. I could have gotten her that house in Jersey she always wanted. Timing can be an asshole. When she had the time, I didn't have the dough. But that's another story.

P.P.S.

Anyways please get rid of any guns you find around the house. I've become very forgetful in old age and have the feeling there are still one or two that need to be discarded. DO NOT KEEP THEM! But my ceramic elephant collection is something you might want. Notice how all the trunks are facing up. That means good luck. You never want them with the trunks facing down. That's bad news. See, you learned something.

P.P.P.S.

Okay so everything I did I did and that's that. Now you be a good boy and take all that money and walk the straight and narrow. It's not always easy but the way to go. Trust me on that one. I wish I could have been around more but you were always in my heart. Maybe this will make up for that at least a little. Maybe not, but I'm hoping it will. Enjoy the elephants.

Squirm

Sky-Touched

Gary feels smited (biblically) though he tells himself he shouldn't. That it's just a matter of being in the wrong place at the wrong time and isn't worth a rotten fig to think otherwise. The clouds after all are machines of science and those jagged volts that crackled down to ravage every cell were just that: *science on the move.*

Mourning Becomes Electric

He meets Frida at a Lightning Strike Survivors support group, sits across from her in a hard brown folding chair. She says to the group, "Forgive me if this sounds harsh, but I don't give a rat's ass about religion." She says this after someone shares that they feel punished and blessed at the same time. "I burned a Bible soon after, at a motel," Frida says. "In the bathtub with a can of lighting fluid. You should have seen it: all those "thees" and "thous" going up in smoke."

They are in a semicircle with their cups of coffee, looking at her, stricken. Gary gets up to hug her. When he touches her sweater he gets a small shock of static electricity and pulls back. Only the two of them know what's happened and laugh. The only person in the group who's been struck by lightning twice gazes at her with a slightly twisted mouth and says, "Damn! Set a Bible on fire in a bathtub. You sure like *playin'* with fire, sister."

Gary is a mattress salesman and late that night at the strip mall he lets Frida in and they bounce on each bed/mattress in a back floor room for "firmness" and "reliability."

"I kind of liked it when they had squeaky bedsprings," Frida says. "When beds talked back."

"You like being bad, don't you?" Gary says.

"Bad is good," she says. "Goody two shoes went flying out of me as I was lying there on the ground unable to move." They are nearly naked, but when he goes to embrace her, she weeps.

After All

"Ever since, you know—it happened—things taste better," Gary tells Frida.

"I know," she says. They are in her studio eating burritos and drinking beer. "You think the electricity is like a really good spice?" She says, smiles.

He half smiles. There is a black bean pressed against his teeth. "No, I mean it. Coming that close to death. Feeling its breath on you, maybe spices things up a bit after, you know?"

"Hmm," she says. Her paintings are all around them on the walls—huge blocks and swirls of color, bold and shooting down the canvases. She tells him how after she was struck she was lost for a time, working at her uncle's music box factory. How the same ditzy tunes kept getting stuck in her head. How it nearly drove her nuts, but then she returned to an early love. She sweeps a hand demonstratively around the room.

He feels foolish when he gives her a nerdy thumbs up. She goes on and on about something or other, and he stops listening but continues nodding.

The rain seems to nail him deeper to the ground, and when he comes to, he tries to move a finger, then two, and then his head, slowly. He is face down in the mud and there is a worm. A worm squirming past his vision. A watery eviction no doubt. It pauses by his face as if to catch its breath. Gary is still disoriented and wonders if he is really alive or … No, it's a fucking worm, you idiot. The thunder is everywhere at once it seems and the searing flashes highlight the worm's slow departure. He wants to scream: "Wait!" But wait for what? It's a worm after all, and not his life, as he knew it, leaving, not his faith, not his old sense of who he was, or why he is. It is just a worm is all. Just one squirmy little wet departure. Nothing more.

"Pass the hot sauce," she says.

"Oh—sure."

Three Entries from a
Somnambulist's Dictionary

Wakethefuckup:

The road trip, they agree, is a last chance. They haven't made love in months, mainly because he drags himself in like a sack of lead fishing weights and plugs, first thing, into cable news. Plugs himself in: brain and breath, and apparently, she concludes: penis (stem to stern as well) and is lost to her.

When she decides to sharpen every knife they own with determined swipes, back and forth against the chef's steel (sitting at the dining room table across from him) he unplugs. Tells her he's an expert in body language and wants to know if there's anything wrong. She is still young-ish and he is still young-ish, and she is keen to that fact. She is wearing a sundress with a floral print and takes her yoga-supple body and does a headstand against the wall. Her dress falls down over her face. She says through several tulips: "Okay, *expert*, what language am I speaking now?"

Finallyshakingthingsup:

Traveling through California they find an away-from-it-all motel with a hot tub and swimming pool situated in an amphitheater of high pines. They are putting on their bathing suits when the room begins to rock a bit. It is their first earthquake experience, and they stand rooted as a framed print of a lake in moonlight tilts on the wall and a Bible on the nightstand slides some. He grabs her hand (with the bathing suit still around his knees) and hops to the bed and they slip under it. The earthquake is a small one, but they remain there. After a time of stillness, they create their own earthquake amid the dust bunnies.

As they lie there in the dark, she tells him how (after her father died) she found an old shoebox of his filled with friction cars. How he was a stern man and picturing him young and playful was alien to her. She told him how she brushed the back wheels again and again against his hardwood floor and watched them, one by one, crash into the walls, and for the first time since he passed, she wept. He comforts her. He shares how he hates his work. All those numbers riotous to him: the emails and cases on the computer blurring at times. Tells her how there are lives represented in those numbers in an avalanche they will never dig out of. "Technology has made us slaves to it," he says, and how he often longs for a simpler time, when the latest technology was *fire*. He smiles. She cannot see it, but feels it. "You know, like smoke signals you saw from a hilltop, or a drum beating out a message in the jungle, like in an old Tarzan movie." She laughs. They both do. She sees him in the dark clearer than she ever has.

Wakethefuckupfuck-up:

They drive to Washington State, are in a rustic lodge bar with elk heads on the walls. They are at a table, a bit drunk, and the subject comes up again about them having a child via a surrogate. She is infertile and they have both, long ago, ruled out adoption. They are financially secure and young enough to parent. The notion of harvesting his sperm and impregnating a surrogate has at times passed by them only as a zephyr. Now it is a music in the wind chimes they both hear. He asks if his sperm being used in that way, growing in someone else, would be okay with her. She nods that it would. "Very much so," she tells him. Then she looks up at one of the elk heads above him on the wall.

"I have a confession," she tells him. "For the last half hour or so, I've had this strong, and I mean *strong* urge to slip out of my panties under this table and toss them onto those antlers." He follows her eyes, turns back. He looks at her for a moment, then laughs hard and long. Her expression doesn't change. After he guzzles some stout, he pats her thigh like a dog under a table. There is a TV on behind the bar tuned to a cable news station. She watches as he turns to watch it, to watch it, to watch it. Then (smeared with a sense of folly) she gazes up at that elk's head. Is drawn to those startled glass eyes peering back at her.

SensationalSaints.com

P.S.

Jennie's into making balloon animals now. You can hear the squeaking rubber as she twists them up in her room. Not just regular ones. Regular animals. She's making extinct ones. Dodo birds, saber-toothed tigers, mammoths … You think it's weird? I mean like do you think it means something? What's wrong with regular animals? I'm just sayin'.

P.S. +

Mike's been coming up with his usual hare-brained schemes for striking it rich since the plant closed. I call it "ghost money" as in it's invisible! I told him instead of striking it rich why don't you try striking it "middle class." That'd suit me just fine.

P.S. ++

My own business is really taking off: *SensationalSaints.com* It's so great working from home. Oh, Pam, there's such a need out there and I'm filling it. When Mike isn't raking in invisible cash he helps. Helps with the molds. I design the figurines, give them their purpose and all (the most important part) and paint them. Saint Serene is my best seller. She's the patron saint of migraines. Who doesn't need her in these crazy times? Saint Woody is another good seller. You pray to him for a bit more action "down there"—guy action. He's a funny looking sort, but you'd be surprised how psychological those problems can be and I get lots of glowing letters. There're plenty more. I'll text you some pics. Saint Hammock is one I'm working on for myself. She's the patron saint of Caribbean vacations. Picture two palm trees with me between in a hammock with a booze-filled coconut I'm slurping down with a straw. Only kidding of course. About the last one, I mean. But then again it's been pretty stressful around here at times (as in *very*), especially with the ghost money and all, so maybe I should add it to the list.

Live Ammo

Live Ammo

You are young. Too young. Too old. Your father is teaching you to hunt. But you do not want to kill anything.

"We'll start off small," your father tells you, "and work our way up." He stands behind you, stooped over, helping you steady the rifle. The squirrel is in your gunsight, stationary, sniffing the air, relying on its ability for swift passage up vertical roadways. Your hands, your arms are shaking and the rifle is swaying in compliance.

"Hold it steady!" your father chides. "Now squeeze the trigger when you've got a clear shot." Your father reaches out a hand to quell the sway, but you jerk away and point the muzzle to the ground and fire. Not once, but again and again. The squirrel jets to a high branch.

"Goddamnit!" your father says, and tears the gun away from you like a scab.

Shoots

You become a freelance photographer. Are good at it. Artsy. *Light* and *nuance* are loyal companions. You do weddings at first to survive, then land jobs here and there for slick magazines. Eventually travel the world for *National Geographic*. Photograph sharks and stingrays, sunken treasure ships with colorful schools of fish circling a deck. High above, you drop from planes like ordinance. Photograph *The Flying Elvises* conjoined in that classic cluster: a merger of ballet and velocity.

You tell the women you meet of your exploits. How you photographed "The Running of the Bulls"—stopped to click your camera, then ran again. Women ask you why you take such chances. Ask about the tattoo they see only a glimpse of, peeking from your shirt across a table by a sea, say: "Could that be …?" They tell you how brave you are. Ask why you live on the edge. They will view the tattoo, in full, soon enough. You feel it is gaudy and misdirected. Hope they will not see what you see.

Oh, Fudge

When you visit your parents, you find your father sitting in his tighty-whities in an inflatable baby pool from your youth he has dragged from the storage shed.

"I'm so embarrassed you had to see him like this," your mother says. "It's gotten worse." So much that was perched on those branches have since scattered. It is not at all hot and the baby pool has only a puddle of water in it.

"You're assholes!" your father says. Your mother darts a look at him. and says, "Oh, fudge!" It is something she has said all your life whenever she disagreed or disapproved. It is sanitized, yet insistent. But now you hear it for the first time as: *"Oh, bullshit!"*

All your father's guns have been gotten rid of as your father had gotten rid of so much else. You look down at your father shriveled and shaking. "Come on Pop," you tell him. "Let's get you out of there and get you something warm to put on." There is a camera on a strap around your neck and you point to it. "I've got another in the truck," you say, and reach a hand out. He stares up at you (new eyes in those old ones cutting through the fog). "Come on," you say, "let's go shoot something."

Close As We Get Sometimes

Moon Dance

There is a steamer trunk filled with sterling silver jewelry by our bed. Mostly charm bracelets from the '40s and silver necklaces with colorful glass pendants attached. It's open like pirate treasure.

My wife and I bid on abandoned storage lockers. Sometimes you get boxes filled with decades old tax returns or a broken typewriter. And then—wham!—you score.

Rita has charm bracelets up to her elbows, and a multitude of necklaces down the front of her, and is dancing. She's singing "What a marvelous night for a moon dance ..." There's actually a luminous moon out, one that peeked in on us earlier. Rita playfully belly dances up to me and shakes her musical arms. I smile, but my attention is elsewhere. She tells me to "lighten up"—returns to our ample haul.

I hold the old boat's log with the reverence it deserves. It's from the late 1800s and fragile. The cover is nearly detached. It was in a small box by itself. I almost dumped it. Didn't pay it any mind till I read the first page, then: wham-o!

Negative Entropy

16 August, 1893
We travel down the muddy river. We have a small crew and a guide who also serves as translator. He is a reedy man with narrow eyes, and the entire expedition rests on his veracity and expertise. Jared and I are hopeful, but keep our expectations restrained as best we can for two scientists on a quest for what some may deem, The Fountain of Youth. "Fountain" is a misnomer of course. It is more likely rare herbs in combination we wish to study. There's a fabled village we've been told exists, where 100 years is a median age and good health prevails. Negative entropy: an interruption in the natural order of "disorder" is what we're after. A disruption in the metabolic aging process on a cellular level ...

Some of the writing is smeared and water stained and the pages are brittle. I hold a magnifying glass over them. There is some script that is impossible to make out and there are pages missing. I think about time, how fast it travels, sandpapers us down. How we dwindle in the end. Even the best moon dancers among us. "A Fountain of Youth." How frigging exciting is that?

"Hey, Sherlock," Rita says (referring to me bent over the magnifying glass), "look at this one." She holds up a charm bracelet. "It's a French poodle between a unicorn and the Eiffel Tower. How's that for a mystery?"

Close As We Get Sometimes

19 August, 1893
The humidity is insufferable and the bugs, heaven help us! And the crocs eyes breaking the waterline, gaping. It's unnerving! Then, a menace unseen, shoots an arrow onto the deck from somewhere onshore. We determine it a warning. But so much is at stake, so much unsettled that we

push on. Our guide is shaken. He speaks something in that odd tongue like an incantation we deduce is akin to prayer ...

I stop reading, can sense how this ends. Like all wild goose chases end. But I want to believe in the *quest*. It's all about the quest, isn't it? Rita is singing louder now with a bottle of wine in hand as she leans over the treasure chest. I put the boat log in the drawer of my nightstand and close it. Rita looks so lovely with her hair down and all that silvery shine about her, you might think she was years younger.

Orange/Door Hinge

Looking Up

Brad digs the hole a bit larger than the length and width of his body (six-ish feet deep). His dog watches from the window, the pane fogging, then clearing, fogging then clearing …

Brad puts a ladder in the hole and climbs down, lies face up gazing at the sky. A bird passes, eventually a plane. There are so many places to take off from and land somewhere else, Brad thinks. The plane appears so small. Distance reduces everything. All those people, those seats and trays, those brains ticking away—this and that, the wings, the fuselage, can fit in the flat of his hand. He's always wanted to travel. To get drunk and dive into a river in Spain. Hell, anywhere else.

A bit of dirt falls onto his face and Brad brushes it aside. He takes out his cell phone and begins calling friends and family, chatting. Never once revealing this new earthy location. He has never felt more alive.

Sweet Williams

He fills the hole back in. Thinks sometimes you just need to shake things up. Thinks of what to plant in the filled-in plot. Perhaps freesias or sweet Williams (some nice smelling life-form). He's pleased with himself that he didn't need to mountain climb some sheer rock, or jump from an airplane with his heart fluttering like a caged bird in a wind storm. He lets Malcolm out and tosses the ball for him. He cannot determine which of them is happier.

Rhyme Time

Brad is a guard in a prison guard "cowboy rap" band. He writes most of the songs, having a facility for rhyming. Finds the clever near rhymes most compelling. There are bleeding jukeboxes, booze-soaked nights, bear traps with platinum hair, hard times blistered and blasted out with staccato cadences as each member takes a turn rapping at their monitoring station, while the others beat on desks and a turned over trash bucket.

But it all comes to a halt when an inmate in one of the cells floods his toilet bowl again in rancorous protest, utilizing this one weapon of outcry. Water is spilling from under the door and off the edge of the tier. It is an unsettling falls of sorts. Brad and his colleagues don their face shields and protective gear for a cell extraction. The inmate is in for a double homicide, so they are not taking any chances.

The prison jumpsuits are all orange, and Brad tries to think of a rhyme for the word *orange*, but can't. As they climb the stairs to the tier, he thinks: *door hinge*, but can't for the life of him, figure out in what context to place it, or in what kick-ass-tellin'-it-like-it-is song with a pounding beat, a wimpy-ass *orange/door hinge* rhyme might ever flourish in Brad's world.

Chickens in the Parlor

Moat In Lieu of a Welcome Mat

When my mother felt her life had become drab and spark-smothered, her lipsticks became redder and redder. And she built a moat around the house. Each day when my father came home from scrubbing graffiti off subway station walls, he'd swim through a clinging storm of mosquitoes to get to the front door with one hand paddling, the other holding his bottle of whiskey above the brine.

Old MacDonald

Mother sprinkled feed on the rug for the chickens in the "parlor" (What she called that tiny room with a convertible sofa in it.) The chickens hopped up onto the furniture knocking things over. I was young and didn't mind their ceaseless pecking. My father found a burial plot inside the newspaper and started digging, so he never noticed the new dress Mother was wearing or the candy apple red high heels. "This is what you get when you act like Old MacDonald," Mother said, sweeping her arm broadly and causing a few chickens to flutter feckless wings. "Ee-i-ee-i-o," she said.

Steam Scream

Mother rid the house of chickens, and Dad learned to cha-cha-cha. (It's strange to think how old they seemed then—how young they really were.) They were in the kitchen dancing when the teapot started screaming. Father turned, but Mother said, "Leave it." That she didn't want to stop for a single minute, that those red high heels were out of their coma. She was wearing a flared sundress and Father had on his grey razor-creased trousers with high cuffs. I found a quarter once in one of those cuffs as they draped over a chair. It was an archeological highpoint.

Father seemed to like the way that dress bell-shaped as she twirled, and the feel of it.—the tea kettle, not so much. A record skipped on the turntable, was stuck in a brassy repetitious snippet over and over … Father turned again, sweating at that point.

"Leave it," Mother said.

Petrified

Split

Clare is married to the town preacher. In church he is a lightning rod for the Lord. Channels His good words to sponges in suits and dresses. At home, she thinks, he is a petulant asshole. Frustrated by that fact (and perhaps combined with her increasing attraction to the organist) she decides to chop down a tree on their wooded property. A tall one. Not out of any sense of symbolism, but merely to sweat his negativity out of her. To separate something so intransigent, so rigidly rooted, unmoved by wind or season. Trees never want to roam. Take vacations. Feel the sun and moon on them from somewhere else. Well, hell, she reconsiders, after the first blow of the ax sinks in, maybe there *is* some bit of symbolism. No matter.

Look Sharp

On the back deck Clare smokes a cigarette. She has incense burning in empty flowerpots on either side of her to mask the smell. Wonders if Jesus ever smoked, and what He would have smoked. A tobacco with some fancy Roman name no doubt. She tries to picture it dangling from one corner of His mouth. Quickly dismantles the image. Inhales deeply. Replaces it with the image of her husband mowing the front lawn that time in his military uniform on Memorial Day. That chaplain's uniform he ironed till the creases were razor-sharp. How embarrassed she was with his chest all rooster-rich and puffed out like that. How she feels sometimes as if she were freeze-dried and waiting for some liberating downpour to stand in.

Organist in Relief

After a sermon, while her husband is outside shaking hands with parishioners, Clare leans over the church organ and flirts with the organist. She has so much to offer in so many ways. The flowers on her dress are bright and full. He seems to notice. She whispers something, sotto voce, not at all intended to be heard.

"Excuse me?" he says. But she glances instead at a stained glass angel sun-lit into fluorescence, then puts a hand softly on his knee and smiles. When he stands she notices his pants fit a bit tighter.

Later she tells her husband she's going to visit her sister, and rents a red convertible instead. Lets the wind tangle her hair, her cigarette smoke fly out into the world unmitigated. When she pulls off to the side of a dirt road she hears a woodpecker going at it. Thinks back to a cartoon she saw as a kid: a woodpecker on a bough with a crumpled beak and a startled expression. Then the view panned down to a sign. It read "Petrified Forest." She didn't get the joke at the time, but laughed anyway, because of the look on the bird's face. All these years later, she smiles when she thinks of it, though sardonically now, not at all sure how any of it could have happened differently.

Slaps Against the Bow

Imagine That

It starts off one night in bed and Mattie says, "Let's pretend we're lost at sea in a small raft. Just the two of us. We're waiting to be rescued and there are sharks in the water. Not necessarily circling, but they're there. You can see the fins now and then and it won't be long before the fresh water runs out."

I put my book down. "Pretend?" I say.

"Yes. More like *imagine.*"

"Why would I want to do that?"

"Okay," she says, "forget about the pretend part. *I want us to see other people.*" And in that moment I notice a fly crawling on the book butterflied on my lap. One of those flies, in late stage, that can no longer fly. Can only crawl. All that is left to it.

How Many?

I take note of her public smiles now with new eyes. I've never
noticed before how many ways there are to smile. How many
muscles must be involved. How much inner can become
outer: fake, patronizing, half-hearted, flirty, lasso, superglue,
calling card, red carpet, beckoning, teasy, a promise, and, oh-
my-god—the promise of a promise kept.

Brine Against the Bow

Mattie comes running in from the garden. We've put up bird
feeders all around the yard. Delighted at the plethora of hummingbirds they've attracted, with their helicopter capacity for
suspending midair to feed. They've given us such pleasure, sitting in our lawn chairs on the deck observing them. But now
one (most likely a protective mother) has flown close to her
face, she tells me. Says it was *menacing*. "The beak on that
thing," she goes on, "could take an eye out—just like that!"
She snaps her fingers.

I open a bottle of wine, pour for the two of us. "I'm not
talking about breaking up," she says (flinging a non sequitur at
me)—"you know that, right?"

"Not right," I say.

"What I mean is: stretching our horizons. Po-ten-tial-ly."

"Potentially?"

"Sure. Maybe we could swing a bit. Something like that. It
might be fun, make our bond even stronger. I try to picture it.
An "Oh, yeah-h" smile is in full bloom this time as some guy
has his hands all over her. Perhaps his wife is doing the same
with me, only my smile is more: "Who the hell are *you*?" This
is out-of-body stuff and there are no flightless flies to distract
me. Only underthings flung this way and that. I snap out of it.

Notice Mattie is wearing a low-cut blouse. Have I stopped no-
ticing such things? Has stasis set in, some insidious novocaine
of familiarity? *Hell!*

Inside I feel like a diminished, paradoxical version of Ahab
biting his fingernails, listening to the displaced seawater slap
against the bow. I gaze at her. Hummingbirds for Chrissake, I
think—dear God, not the fucking hummingbirds!

Rodeo Clown

Chicken on a Chain

The bull torpedoes out of the chute: a bulky ballet of heft and violence. The rider tries to move with the sudden shifts and bucks for as long as he can, finally flung to the ground, as Roland and three other rodeo clowns race toward the animal, all horns now, six feet wide it seems/six feet under, potentially. They circle like hornets: a buzz of expletives, wild hands pestering the bull into distraction. Their colorful tear-away garments in a blur giving the rider a chance to retreat. The barrel clown running closer waving his arms, the bull exiting the small disconcerting dust devils it finds itself in the middle of— the crowd cheering when the rider jumps the fence with only a throbbing shoulder and one fractured pinkie finger.

Head in Hand

Roland is in a gorilla suit at a kid's birthday party. He was once a headliner. But too many shattered bones and joints on fire later, here he is. A skeleton after all needed to stay intact more times than not to serve as a viable fitting dummy for that sinewy cowboy body. Now he peers out of holes in a matted gorilla head at the kids squealing as he knuckle-scrapes the ground and occasionally takes selfies with the parents.

Later, behind a shed, holding the gorilla head in one hand, a drink in the other, Laura Jean lights cigarettes for the two of them. Roland smiles that familiar lop-sided smile as she says, "Damn, Roland, now don't you still look like a thousand gallons worth of pride in a ten-gallon hat."

His

Roland visits some bull ranches. The oxys he takes hardly work anymore. Maggie is back home with the kids, and a cold beer and some cold pizza will be there for him. The small bit of cash he has left from his heyday he'll put toward a bull with a few other investors. (Hopefully a star—a superstar bull like "Chicken on a Chain" or a dozen others. He stays up nights thinking of names waiting for the drugs to kick in, pictures that lunging fury, that near aerobatic mayhem. He writes down: "Spring-Loaded"—listens for the rodeo announcer's amplified voice in his head, the crowd clapping, whistling through their teeth. He puts a pencil to his lips, writes: "Captain Crush," then scratches it out. Maggie stops breathing, then gasps for air in her sleep beside him. He gives her a little nudge and she turns over on her side and goes back to snoring. She refuses to wear that damn sleep apnea mask that makes her look like she's headed for the moon.

"Better Think Twice" he jots down, imagines sinew in bulk shooting out, poundage in ruptured air and dirt. And it will be *his*. He hears the cheering crowd, the announcer revving them up—the adulation. He clicks off the lamp. It all sounds so good in the dark. Most things don't. And there's that lopsided smile again.

The Small End of the Funnel

P.S.

Hey, guess what? Brenda's doing Phone Sex. Can you believe it? I remember her saying the word "robust" once. It was hot!

My Kay's into photography now. Close-ups of rusty staples in phone poles. A red spider on a yellow sponge. Artists. Christ!

P.P.S.

I called Brenda last night. And man oh man!

P.P.P.S.

Out of nowhere Kay says, "All cheaters should be pushed down a funnel with the small end in hell." I looked at her like, that's interesting. Like, there's nothing in *this* fridge worth taking. Only began breathing again when she started taking pictures of the cat.

Late Blooming Gigolo

Scents

Earl was a professional bingo caller. Had the temperament/the flair for it. Turned to that gallery of hopefuls with his random edicts. Drawn to Rita (regal Rita) inevitably. Her scents of perfume and want. That pearl necklace and her dignified air. The diamond broach and the voracity with which she laid out so many cards with a widow's privilege. That Siren call: "*Bingo!*"

Cents

He, her Ulysses, sans the rocks to crash against, only that gold in manageable chunks/that want/that fire to warm against. He wouldn't give two cents to change any of it.

Sense

"B-17, O-23, N-9 …"

The scratches into his back, those long candy-apple-red fingernail markings under his shirt, even when it was so hot his shirt stuck to him, unseen. Their secret.

Earl, whose prior life, so helter-skelter—Big Earl with four firecrackers and a cigarette between his lips, asking for a light. Before. His life, like that. Someone else entirely now. Just a cigarette now at the corner of his mouth. Perhaps one of those fancy French ones which stunk up the room in all the right ways—edgy, Bohemian. And, *Holy Good Lord God Almighty*, his life was finally beginning to make sense.

The Antiquity of Certain Moments

A New Weather

After Glen comes back from the war he notices Leanne's love-making style is different. Little things here and there. That, and she's taken up roller skating. Seriously devoted to it. She even goes skating down their long hall, back and forth along the hardwood floor.

"Do you have to?" he says. But she has her earbuds in and is immersed in a raucous music. He is trying to read by the window. Has a bad ear from a blast during a battle, and sometimes things sound like gibberish because of it or different than what is intended. "I'm going out," is heard as: "It's snowing out." She is always going out it seems. And it is always snowing out, and *in* at times. Those icy landings on bare skin. It isn't the snow that bothers him, that is pretty enough—it's the slush which follows.

Speed Lines

He's doing demolition, wants to open up the living room. A wall stands in the way. Leanne's taken to drawing stick figures on it in the meantime. Mostly characters on roller skates with little speed lines behind the wheels. A sledgehammer dangles from his hand as Glen looks more closely. One of the stick figures is wearing a dress (a triangle) and has little inverted triangles for breasts. The speed lines are darker than any of the others, as if she's gone over them. Glen goes into the steamed up bathroom where she is painting her lips: a color he's never seen before called, Blushing Devil Red. She's wiped out a clear circle in the fogged up mirror. "I'm going out," she says. His one good ear is facing her and he hears it correctly. He turns and walks away. The sledgehammer sinks into the wall, the war swings into the wall, those ridiculously juvenile "tit pics" she's been sending him on his phone explode into the plaster—those speed lines, that Blushing Devil Red ...

Screech

He drives to the beach, looks up at a flock of pelicans flying through what is left of some skywriting. Can only make out a few fading words. He sits by the shore and lights a cigarette. He's only recently started up again. An intrusive thought rises: a jagged ankle bone in a combat boot. The boot standing straight up without anything else attached. He blots it out, replaces it with one of those many immature tit pics Leanne sends him, wonders if they were even intended for him, or if she is functioning off of some displaced momentum. He becomes suddenly aware of the antiquity of certain moments. Like crazed china, somehow old in an instant.

A seagull screeches, and then there are the waves, their steady rhythm. That is the music he wants to hear. His phone dings. Most likely some more guilt pics. He doesn't respond. A seagull lands at the water's edge It has one foot missing, yet it appears perfectly balanced—a few feathers ruffled by wind. "Hello, brother," Glen says.

Visits to the Underworld
(East Harlem, NY, 1957)

Rental Service

For a time my mother rented out our living room to a mobster so he could have his occasional "sit-downs" in a safe location. We lived in an old tenement building and every now and then without notice, he'd knock gently, and he and one or two men would nod as they entered. My mother paid them no mind and mostly tooled around the kitchen finding busy work. The kitchen was adjacent to the living room separated only by a sheet tacked over the doorless entrance, and you could see their big shadows as they leaned into each other in whispers or stood up and shook hands.

When it was time for the mobster to leave he'd reach deep into a pocket and pull out a roll of cash and peel away some bills and hand them to my mother. He'd tousle my hair without saying anything and they'd leave.

One time he came to the door and handed my mother a rifle wrapped in a large beach towel. We kept it behind our convertible sofa. After a while someone I never saw before came to retrieve it and handed my mother an envelope. No words were spoken. Then the mobster stopped coming, and word spread that his body was found in the East River. The sofa never felt right with that secret behind it, and even after the secret was removed. It was always a bit creepy: that big gun in that pretty towel—the ghost of it still there.

A Hole in the Head in the Hole

We were digging in the ruins of the old bathhouse (from another era in Jefferson Park) in the dirt between the rubble, when we found the skull. We'd dug up Indian Head pennies there before, and back then any kind of penny was a treasure. The skull was human. Just like in the movies or on a box of poison. It looked like a rock at first. Then it took shape, that creepy shape, and we jumped back. Once we gathered ourselves, we removed the surrounding dirt, and there it was staring back at us from those hollow sockets. I held it for a moment, then dropped it as though it might turn and bite me. Petey picked it up and noticed it had a hole in the back of it. It drew us in, that hole. It was before kids said, "cool" all the time, but our eyes said: "cool." I put a finger to the hole and then we both did. We rubbed the dirt from it. Poked our fingers through the sockets. It was weird and wonderful. It was "ours."

But Petey said if he took it home and his father found it, he'd beat him. I said if my mom found it, she'd hit me with it, then fling it out the window. It was nearly a pet now we were rubbing it so much. Sadly though we decided to put it back. We covered it up and dug some more far from it. Found three pennies and played eeny-meeny to see who'd get the odd one. The pennies lay meaningless in our pockets as we rambled on about everything, but, on the way home. They'd lost their charge and there was no getting it back again.

Cold Storage

We were walking on the dark side of the street along the iron fence bordering the park when we heard the banging. Then the muffled sounds of someone trying to speak. It sounded distant and frenzied: "Muum-uhngg ...

John-Boy was a year older than Petey and me and he always let us know it. "What the fuck?" he said. There was no one. We were on our way to a sewer grate in the park behind the baby pool to hunt down some *scalaboons*. Those giant water bugs from Hell that rose up out of the dank depths of the sewer. An army of them. John-Boy had his stickball bat and we'd trade off beating them into paste before they had a chance to fly up and crawl in our hair or up our pant legs. The banging grew louder and we kept looking around, even in the bushes just beyond the iron fence. Nothing. We walked a bit further, and there it was. Coming from the trunk of a maroon Chevy. John-Boy put a finger to his lips and we stopped.

"Mmmbb, garrrrh ..." Bang, bang, bang ... It got louder as we approached.

"Holy shit," I said. "You think we should call the cops?"

John-Boy raised his bat and put it over his shoulder. "You fucking nuts. You wanna wind up in there too?" I didn't need for him to explain that. The street had rubbed off on us. I chalked it up to a mental lapse.

Out of nowhere, with the absurdity of someone tapping on a giant turtle shell, Petey knocked on the trunk. "You fucking idiot. Why'd you go and do that for?" John-Boy said. Petey shrugged.

"Let's split," I said.

We were about to run when we heard a man, a very big man I'd seen around the neighborhood, yell, "Hey!" There was a row of old tenements across the street. Two men came out of one of them. I didn't recognize the other, smaller man. They both approached us quickly.

"Don't run," John-Boy whispered. The big man who called out was over us in no time. The muffled grunting and banging kept getting louder.

"I know you kids," the big man said. The other guy was staring us down with a hand in his pocket. "You kids lost or something?" the big man said.

"What? John-Boy said. "Huh? Huh?"

"You a fucking wiseass?" the big man said.

"No," John-Boy told him, "We just can't hear too good. None of us can. You might even say we're all deaf."

The two men looked at each other, smiled. "Deaf can be a good thing sometimes," the big man said. "Who knows, maybe someday when you're old enough I'll buy you all hearing aids." The two of them laughed and got into the car. "Now fuck off," the big man said as a parting endearment and we did. Were happy to. There were always the scalaboons waiting for us with their creepy-crawly hard shells to crack open, there were plenty of stoops we could sit on and shoot the shit, there were all those words and shivers banging around inside of us like that guy in the trunk. But none of us dared let them out.

"I'm heading home," John-Boy said.

"Me too," I said.

"Me too," Petey said.

And that was the end of it.

Birdcage

Ribcage

Margaret has an old medical student skeleton dangling in her studio she purchased online. To her it does not look Halloween-ish, but rather, pragmatically, she views it as the hidden vehicle we drive/drives us. If it were a birdcage (the ribcage) in a marriage, she thinks, it would be a perfect one. A place to perch/a place to launch from.

Shadow Piano

When she was young (a hippy) hitchhiking beside a stand of poplars, she played shadow piano with her feet on the long shadows they cast. Hopping about from one to the other. The music in her head, not Rachmaninoff, but just as fierce. "You're weird," said the young man that was with her at the time (she now, with all the surrounding details missing) thinks of as Blackie: thick black hair, black beard, clinging black chino pants. (From a time when "weird" was a good thing.)

Charles is cooking bacon, and she likes the sound of its spitting choreography. He is a good husband, she tells herself. The small potted plants on the sill in the kitchen cast shadows (a jazzy mix of various shapes and lengths) she does not think to play.

Skeleton

At their wedding party, Margaret was so drunk her skeleton betrayed her, pitching this way and that. When she puked on the folded wings of an ice-sculptured swan, Charles took her in his arms as though nothing had happened. Slow walked her to the dance floor. (Whispered something she has since forgotten.) Pressed her close and led her in a slow (old honey leaving a spoon, slow) dance to the racy music playing in her head.

Songbird Among the Serpents

Haiku in a Can

He does not have a smoking gun tattoo or LOVE and HATE inked into the knuckles of each hand. He does not have a tattoo at all, or belong to a gang. Yet he works his spray paint can beside the inscrutable gang tags on the wall—hieroglyphics of territory and terror. *His* graffiti with ready translation: haiku, his own, a songbird among the serpents. Surrounded by *the Dead Eye Boys, The Fourth Street Outlaws*—their scrawls.

He refers to the words written in ink on the palm of his hand and along his arm. His spray can hisses against the stone:

> from the distant porch
> a cigar tip brightens—
> crickets, stars

Dissertation on Snow

He visits his parents' trailer home. His mother is in the micro garden out front, tending the freesias she inhales the scent of like a drug. She is behind the white picket fence she always wanted, downsized somewhat the way her life is. His father is bug-eyed before a 60" TV only a few feet away in the miniature living room. Says he misses the old test patterns on TV they used to have at the end of the night. Says they were pretty like sand paintings. Sand paintings in a snowstorm. He laughs. "Not real snow of course, but you wouldn't know about that. Just a lot of TV dots dancin' around on the screen ..." His son listens, nods. He needs money for more spray paint. There is poetry waiting in each can he shakes. "Can I borrow 20 bucks?" the boy asks when his father stops to take a breath.

Hats and Haiku

Poetry is everywhere, the boy thinks. Even in a favorite uncle's closet. His bald uncle's hat collection. Those many hats he wore like a peacock would with its flared out plumes. Every style and color. He wore them even in the house. Even during those last weeks in bed, a fedora, the boy recalled. And his uncle understood the value of words, and asked the boy to read them aloud to him to the end.

Tonight the boy is by a playground wall marked, lavishly, with gang graffiti. It's late. He shakes the can. Finds a big clear patch of cement framed by gangster tags and lewd drawings. He runs track in high school. He is fleet-footed, an asset, but not faster than a bullet. He'd be faster than a knife blade or any chasing legs. He knows all the exit routes.

He sprays large black letters:

> sunny day—
> sleeping under the lawn chair,
> a white cat, checkered

Then:

> in the old museum—
> at the foot of the t-rex
> a dead fly ...

He stops, listens like a meerkat or a deer. He shakes the can, shakes the can. He can hear it, pressurizing, the pulsing paint rising up inside it.

Black Bananas

P.S.

Good grief! He has his parrot speak to me over the phone. "Hot momma," it says in that creepy high-spirited screech and I can hear him faintly prompting it in the background.

P.P.S.

I was sitting in the kitchen the other day staring at the black bananas. He keeps bringing over bunches of bananas. The potassium he says. That he needs the potassium. He plops them in my grandmother's etched Depression glass bowl. You know that beautiful light green one I showed you. I hate bananas and they always wind up turning black by the time he comes back over. He tells me not to dump them, that they're just right for banana nut bread that way and that you can still get the potassium and he'll give me his mother's secret recipe. Which he never does. Like I'd really give a hoot if he did.

P.P.P.S.

Lately when he calls he starts off in that high pitched parrot's voice trying to be funny: What's up buttercup? What's up buttercup? I don't even fake laughing anymore. I just do whatever it is I'm doing. My nails, or watching TV or whatever. Remind myself whenever I need to that you take the good with the bad sometimes. He actually likes opera and has season tickets. He cries at the same movies I do. The same parts. He tries to hide it but I can tell. And well, the sex. Let's just say I ain't complaining. But the parrot thing and the potassium thing have got to go. There are fruit flies circling Grammy's gorgeous bowl now and we just can't have that. There are some things where you just have to draw the line!

Headlines

WOMAN TERRORIZES FISH!

After Ellie throws the steam iron at Mel (the fact that it is still plugged in saving him grave bodily insult) he knows it is over. She calls him a "sham." A *sham*, he thinks. Ha!—good one! He knows she's been sneaking around with that fake little man from Accounts Pending with his elevator shoes and padded shoulder sports jackets.

She runs over and snatches his clip-on bowtie (as if it were an ill-gotten badge of honor) and tosses it into their fish tank, freaking out the angelfish for a moment. But they simply swim around it as the leviathan sinks down and slowly settles on a mermaid sitting on a pirate's treasure chest in blue sand. If only his troubles were as easily circumvented, Mel thinks.

MAN FINDS HIMSELF IN A CROWD!

Post-divorce Mel becomes a wedding singer. He'd always had a fair enough singing voice and an affinity for working a crowd. His cousin has a connection with a band and they pair up. "Moon River" has couples all melting into each other on the dance floor, and for once Mel feels like *somebody*—a head-liner. In control. Not like a puppet master kind of control, but more like an all-grown-up Cupid with musical rhymes in lieu of arrows. He has lots of opportunities with the unspoken-for friends of the various brides smiling up from their chicken fricassee. And, like the carved ice swans and peacocks, enjoys a tenuous commitment to form and reliability.

MAN DISCOVERS SOMETHING BIGGER THAN HIMSELF!

Time squeezes Mel like a winepress with none of the beneficial outcomes. He is no longer able to keep up with the ballroom bookings and pressures and takes to drink. He tries to sell his "genetic substance" to a sperm bank, but is rejected. He has never wanted his own kids, but now, hearing Ellie has one with "The Shrimp" he does. Has a newfound hunger for line-age. He gets two dogs and a cat. The cat terrorizes the two small dogs that hide under his bed.

Eventually, he meets up with a raucous group of men he finds online. They gather once a week at a beer garden, and sing, robustly, old whaling songs, swinging their arms and spilling their stout. They are a hearty bunch with anchor tat-toos and gusto. You can almost feel the sea mist after the third or fourth drink and Mel's learning to enjoy community some-what: the high-fives and fist bumps, the occasional dirty lim-erick. But, hell, he still misses Ellie and wishes her and The Shrimp's child were "theirs." And, damn, damn, damn—he feels sorry for the whales.

A Sky Full of Crickets

Hatching

They are strapped in their upside-down car for hours before the firemen, slicing into it, free them. The deer comes out of nowhere and when Clyde swerves the car sharply, it flips. The airbags release, with a moment's harsh embrace, then deflate. When Arleen says: "Fuck!" in a tone familiar to him, he is finally able to breathe again.

Bottom's Up

Arleen has a limp for many months after the accident and he has a hard time opening and closing his right hand and lifting his arm over his head, which they consider a minimal, if not a miraculous consequence. In the upside-down car with the blood rushing to his head and the silence quickening his heart, he looks over at his wife and screams her name. Then her eyes spring open and she blurts out: "Fuck!" He tries the door. It no longer is a car door, but a locked vault. "Try yours," he says, as she reaches down and brings up a red wet hand from her ankle.

He is not particularly religious but he begins to bargain with the sky (empty or otherwise) through the bottom of the car, his roof now. Not knowing if there is anything beyond it, but the crickets' scraping chirps or the insistent scent of a skunk a half-mile away. He decides to hedge his bets.

Tomahawk Peace Pipe

Part of the deal he makes (he presumes) with the crickets, is to transition from hard liquor to beer, and then to ween himself off drink altogether.

Now they are on vacation in Mexico. He agrees to spend the day gift shopping and gives Arleen two days' worth of back massages in exchange for taking her to a bullfight. She thinks the picador is handsome, before he sticks his colorful lances into the bull. He had, she felt, a stately look about him on his stately horse prior. Now she sees something else: a cruel, unfeeling look that perhaps was always spring-loaded. Cruel/stately—she begrudges them being so interchangeable. Like the tomahawk peace pipe Clyde bought online. Which was it after all?—something to split a head open, or a smoky handshake?

Clyde holds his beer in his uninjured hand. There is a small flask of whiskey in the breast pocket of his jacket.

"You're drinking too much again," Arleen says.

"Hemingway," he tells her. "This is our day. Me and *Papa*."

The Matador's sword goes in, and she turns away. The bull buckles to its knees. Clyde shoots up with the crowd and cheers. Blood spills out into the dirt.

"Hemingway's dead," she says, but he is lost amid the crowd's, and his own, stormy applause. The flask is just above his heart (right where he wants it). He can feel it pounding there.

Three Tarot Cards Reimagined

The Piano Dancer

He is a blind piano tuner and he comes highly recommended. He arrives early. Grace determines he must have been blind all or most of his life, for he has an easy way about him, tapping about, only asking basic directions. She's just recently gotten out of the shower and is in her robe. It is just an old spinet piano from her youth. A kind of torture device in her mother's hands. But now that her mother has passed, it is hers to create as many misdirected finger-walks as she wishes.

She watches him for a while making adjustments, turning tuning pins this way and that—tap, tap, tapping the keys. Notes his slender frame. So unlike Fred's. Fred with his signature on her walking papers. Fred, who felt the syntax of heavy hands on her his best penmanship.

The piano tuner has a thin mustache and she wonders how he could have trimmed it so precisely. These are a very different set of hands. When he finishes tuning the piano, he begins playing, expertly, in a variety of genres: classical, jazz, pop ... Turning the spinet into a grand piano. She feels safe with him, she in the light of day and he in that curtained world. She begins dancing, bare-footed on the rug. Lets her robe swing open a bit, feeling free, invisible. But when he says, "You smell fresh," she stops midway into a twirl, and somehow finds, even an acute olfactory reveal, unsettling. Tightens her sash.

The Fire Master

The Fire Master slides the cans from the hinged flaps behind the basecamp outhouse with an iron hook, arranges them in a semicircle. The cyclone of black flies are everywhere, their frenzied bustling in mismatched orbits above the foul bottom halves of 55-gallon drums, traversing the red bandana he wears to shield himself against the smoke/the stench. He is attached to the forward medical combat unit in this strange country/this hellishly surreal construct. He pours diesel fuel into the cans, his one revenge against the pestering storm that has gathered. He tosses a match into each can and backs away. The flames quickly rage in swirling force. He pulls down his bandana below his chin and lights a joint. The flies are either incinerated or off somewhere nearby, waiting. He can be seen through the wavering heat, undulating somewhat, and with a trick of the eye, he is on fire too. Soldiers nod from a distance as they pass, head for the dispensary, the Quonset hut wards. It is something out of Dante's Inferno. One of the "circles" not yet numbered. From behind the wards you can hear the medevac chopper blades whip as they hover like giant dragonflies, coming and going. They leave light, fly over the tree lines. Come back with their bellies full.

The Face Wizard

Each line, contour, eye shape, sharp/round/square chin, thin, thick lips, an expression, tattoo, hairstyle, skin tone … The police composite artist digs—it is an excavation through the rubble. Archaeological. There is nuance. There are shadows and depth. The screams, loud or muffled in the room. The ghost of them haunting his sketch pad. He hears them: the galloping heartbeats, the footsteps approaching, departing. "Okay," he says in a soft voice, realizing how the breath can shatter like a teacup. "Was his nose like any of these?" He holds up a sheet of examples encased in plastic. "I know it's hard, but try. Just point to one, even if you're not sure. When we're done we can make adjustments." He wants to provide adjustments. That is what was stolen in real time. Brutally canceled out. What he offers. The time to make adjustments.

Brain Waves

Mass Exodus

A spider crawls out of my son's old saxophone in the basement. Such a quiet exodus from such a noisy instrument. A quiet exodus for each of them: my wife, my son in college, this spider. It rappels down on a barely visible line, so light, so light.

Healing Sounds

I visit a "Healing Sounds" therapist. What the hell? There is the use of sacred instruments and voice tones to free the boulders that have "impacted my spirit." *Brain waves* are mentioned again and again. I close my eyes as gongs and voice tones "reconfigure the molecules" surrounding me. But a silly thought, born of cynicism, emerges despite my best urgings at suppression. *Brain waves,* I think, and picture brains coming in with the tide, their slippery convolutions catching the light just so (an ocean's-worth, rising/falling in the froth). I smile, a faux appearance of bliss belied by the shouts in my head: *erase! erase!*

Light Enough

I am old enough to remember (as a kid) radio was the movie theater of the mind. How what you imagined made it so. The way books still are. I look out the window at the sky. I wonder if there are books in Heaven (mysteries, no doubt). Wonder if they play cards up there. Or have pets, for that matter, and if they strafe at fleas. Eternity after all is a fairly long time and you'd need something to do. Maybe one could learn to play an instrument (a loud one, say) start a garage band. Or does one just float around all day in outer space, remembering, or just hang out lower down on a cloud, like on the ceiling of the Sistine Chapel? Light enough to not fall through. Like the rain.

The Twins

Stereophonic

Grandfather told the twins there was a man at the door with a gun. Joey ran to the door, Jerry in tow. There were two Jehovah's Witnesses in neat blue suits standing there. One of them was holding a small black Bible.

"No thanks," the twins said in unison. They did that a lot, especially when watching TV. "The stereo brothers," their mother would say.

"Poor Grandpa," Jerry said, monophonically.

Twin Years

The twins climbed up onto the billboard platform off the freeway. Sat under a beautiful woman's enormous smile, a diamond's glint radiated from a few toothpaste-scrubbed front teeth. They passed a joint back and forth. Joey was five minutes older, and in "twin's time" felt that each minute was equivalent to a year's worth. Jerry told him those kinds of differences only worked with dogs: one dog year being equal to seven human years.

"I came out first, I'm older," Joey said. Jerry turned, looked up at that gigantic billboard smile.

"I feel like she could chew me up and spit me out," Jerry said.

"See what I mean?" Joey said.

The Accident

They were at the edge of a cliff overlooking the sea. A ship slowly dotted off toward the horizon. Their legs hung over the ledge. A week earlier, two of their friends played Russian roulette behind the bowling alley with a grandfather's war trophy Luger. They found Philly against the wall with skull bits, brains, and blood all over him, said later to the police it was all about seeing who had the biggest balls.

"My balls are just the right size," Joey said when they discussed the "accident."

"Mine too," Jerry said.

Then, "Wow," they said in unison, as the tip of a blood-orange sun entered the sea.

Boarding Passes

Sizzle

The father keeps bringing home small religious booklets: rectangular shearings with biblical heft. Laughing with his friends, the boy counts out the pills. Uses the colorful pages to roll his joints—Jesus, along with half a dozen talk balloons, sizzling toward his lips.

Banana Roses

At the intervention the boy waves everybody off like pestering gnats (the dense storm of them) as they read parables from their personal *Book of Flames*. The mother telling the story of the young boy who used to peel back the cut end of a banana into a yellow flower he'd give her. "Christ," the boy says.

Maps to Each

Later, when the father speaks to him of Heaven and Hell, handing out maps to each, the boy pulls up his shirt and points to the Sacred Heart of Jesus tattoo (with little drops of tattoo blood, seeping out) spanning his chest. The crucifix tattoo is on his shoulder with God-bright radiating lines surrounding it. "Ink!" the father says.

Musings at the Maw of the Great Abyss or Perhaps Merely a Gopher Hole

The Fates

The computer came flying out the window of an apartment building I was passing and crashed with an end-of-the-world disassembling. It landed a couple of feet in front of me. I put on the brakes. Just seconds earlier I'd been taken with a pair of lovely legs swinging out of the back of a stretch limo, and slowed my gait. What if I hadn't? Did it all hinge on the Fates? Their whims? Perhaps goddesses like their "close calls" as much as "X" marks the spot preordained sad endings. I heard loud voices coming from a floor high up and hurried on, wasn't going to wait and see if a wedding gift toaster or a flatware shower was next.

Satan in a Warden's Suit

We'd found the old school bus rotting in a field. Went inside and made love amid the rust and wildflowers growing up through breaks in the metal. Afterwards we smoked a cigarette we shared like a joint, only because we didn't have a joint to smoke. We were both hippies, young, and a new and ill-defined world stared us down.

"What I don't get," she said, "is why these holy rollers keep putting down the Devil. He's actually a holy man."

She was always saying stuff like that, off-the-wall and out of nowhere. Stuff that made your head explode. Little things, and not so little things that knocked stuff over. She was smarter than me, and I knew it.

"How you figure?"

"Well, think about it. If the Devil is really as bad as they say, then why would he punish people for doing bad things? You'd think he'd reward them instead. It'd be party time down there. But the Devil fries 'em like he was God's warden or something. You know? For doin' God's dirty work for him."

"Wow, I never thought about it that much," I told her. Picked a wildflower from a crack in the floorboard and put it in her hair, at an angle, a few inches deep. About as deep as I was back then.

Asbestos Feet

At the spiritual retreat we learned how to control our breathing, steady our regurgitating minds. Learned how small we were in all that "bigness." If we were fire-breathing dragons, they'd have us believe, we'd only emit a match-worth each. I thought at the time my fire could reach the clouds and cause them to sizzle. It didn't matter how true that was, it only mattered that it mattered. We didn't speak for two days. And I found that silence a kind of scream. When I was alone I fractured the air around me with whispered expletives. It was a trapdoor I slipped down.

The last night, the big last night, under stars large and bright enough to "light the way," we were told we were ready to walk on fire. Hot coals (a narrow strip of them). If we *believed* our tender feet would not be harmed, they assured us, then they would not be harmed. There were asbestos feet in the offing. One by one the acolytes walked across the hot coals glaring up at us like smoldering red devil eyes. When they reached the end, elated and unscorched, everyone cheered. When my turn came I screamed out a banshee alarm, only a few inches in. I jumped off to the side howling and shamed. Where were my asbestos feet? Mine were everyday, mortal feet all along. And the stars there were not so big and luminous after all, I decided. The fluorescent lights at the ER were much brighter.

Lip-Reader

Sidebar

Her/his hands are in aerial abundance, maneuvers nearly balletic above their respective menus. A quiet sidebar at the edge of the storm, where cows and chickens of chatter peripherally wind-fly by, the slats of an old barn, a roof lifted as easily as someone tipping a hat.

Lips

She is the only one of them that can lip-read. Turns from the smile of his own lips to the silent blather of others: "the cheating asshole," lips, "the boss who wouldn't know a decent day's work if it bit him on the ass," lips, "the husband who acts like he's wearing a suit of armor to bed (a rusty one at that)," lips …

There's a ruby tea light candle holder between them, and she watches as his hands make the flame inside it sway with the small wind they create. He tells her how he likes her hair, her necklace. His hand gestures and the small swaying flame say: "Is that jade?"

Vibrations

They point at open menus when the waiter comes. The waiter says: "Good choices." Then catches himself, and only she understands. She tells the man across from her, she just met on rightforthenight.com, that she loves to dance, but doesn't mention (without any clothes on), and how she turns the music way up. How the vibrations profoundly move her to moving. He signs that, unlike her, he used to hear it once, every note, and now it's not the same so he doesn't turn it on. It doesn't turn *him* on. She makes a determination then, and looks away. But after that deeper silence, he taps her arm, tells how he's recently purchased chicken flavored toothpaste for the three-legged dog he rescued from the pound, his softer movements reflected in the flame. With her hands on the table she listens. Decides she likes his tie.

The Penalty of Silence

P.S.

I know you think I'm just a tramp, a slut, a hussy, a floozy, a tart, a loose woman, a scarlet woman, a woman of ill repute, a trollop, a harlot, a flirt, a whore, a strumpet, a wanton, a fallen woman, a nympho, an adulteress, a two-timing cheat … for going elsewhere for affection. Woo, I'm devastated—I DON'T THINK SO!

P.P.S.

When you treat someone like they don't exist, what do you expect? Most times it was like you were wearing antlers to bed. Like a moose. Same difference. What's a gal to do?

P.P.P.S.

So, here's what "I" think. You're a creep, a jerk, a flake, a nut job, a kook, a bonehead, a halfwit, a nincompoop, a block-head, a buffoon, a dunce, a dud, a dolt, an ignoramus, a cretin, an imbecile, a dullard, a moron, a simpleton, a dope, a ninny, a dimwit, a nitwit, a dumbo, a dummy, a dumbbell, a loon, a jackass, a numskull, a birdbrain, a boob ... for putting me through all that deadly silence and neglect for all those years and now for making me burn out my eyeballs looking through this damn thesaurus just to set the record straight!

Little Race Cars

Fins

My cousin, Peter, wins the lottery. Millions. We fought as kids over who would get the little grey (or was it silver?) race car we'd glide across the board when we played *Monopoly*. I don't know if either of us truly wanted it, or if we merely wanted what the other wanted. Now he's got a vintage Cadillac Eldorado. Its shark fins glistening out of his garage. He keeps the garage door open. The car doesn't fit all the way inside. He's getting a new house he says and that Cynthia is leaving him (his wife of twenty-two years). The parties he's been having: the strange new "friends" he invites, she says, are freaking out the cats. And that she's had it. Up to here! The money be damned. But also reminds him she's got a good chunk of it coming. And the cats are going with her and he can have the "birdbrains"—the lot of them. "What?" she tells him, "you think those bimbos are in it for your good looks?" Peter finds her suitcase, he tells me, open on the bed, a vibrator in the corner beside a pile of her lacey bras—a declaration of independence and implication. The suitcase is like a giant maw. He translates: "Adios, asshole!"

Hot Chocolate

Peter ran the concession stand at the skating rink in town where hot chocolate was the big seller. Now he gets calls from all sorts with syrupy voices. Even inventors, he tells me, looking for backing. One wanting him to invest in a Mr. and Mrs. Potato Head spin-off, giving them press-in genitalia. Said they could be used by parents and teachers for Sex Ed in a non-threatening way. "How much they trying to soak you for?" I say into the phone. He says, "Hey, wait a minute. I gotta take this." When he gets back on he says, "You won't believe the pair …" "Stop!" I tell him. He still thinks I want that little race car zooming around the board with me in it. And maybe I do (a little) but mostly I don't. We've got a fireplace, two cars that fit in the garage, a cat that is not freaked out by strange new hands, and the "Scottie dog," the "top hat" and the "thimble" pieces scoot around that Monopoly board as fast as any race car, and with none of the crashes.

Hot Chocolate Again

At his new place Peter tells me he's depressed. "I don't know who to trust anymore," he says. "You know a fake orgasm when you hear one, and that's all I hear anymore. I miss Cynthia and the cats, and goddamnit, a good cup of hot chocolate." He looks at me with a deep, earnest gaze: "How you doing? You short on cash?" he asks. When I tell him I'm all set, he hugs me, and we do our special handshake: elaborate and dorky, just like we did as kids. Back then he'd tell these meandering, longwinded jokes, he'd hear from his parents, and when you were totally exhausted and waiting for a redeeming punchline, he'd never get it right. But I always hoped he'd get it right. "Got any new jokes?" I ask. "Yeah, my life," he says, clicking on a TV nearly as large as the wall across from us.

His Ink and Miss Atomic Bomb

Tats

All his stories, he said, were written in his ink. There was even a tattoo under his full head of hair she'd never seen, but glimpsed the shadow of. She fingered the ones on his chest and thought it peculiar and amusing how some curly black hairs poked through them in the oddest places.

Miss Atomic Bomb

Her great aunt was Miss Atomic Bomb in the 1950s. She showed him a photo of her in a bathing suit, young and beautiful—a mushroom cloud crown on her head. A bunch of grinning soldiers gathered around. Said how she died at 90—left behind over a hundred Chia Pets. The withered plant life browning in their decorative planters her family dumped. Had no real pets. Imagined Miss Atomic Bomb as a tattoo added to his picture book body, had it been *his* aunt. Ever young—flourishing for as long as he did.

Thicket

In the diner, she couldn't help staring at the creature clawing out of his collar, cinched by a dark tie cutting into his neck. Wore it for a job interview he was back from. Wondered what its story was, and the prison ones too. The crude spook show tats, shiny when he got out of the shower. When he took her and she was among them. That thicket. Unlike her husband's blank canvas. Across from her on one hand: LOVE. On the other: HATE. A letter for each knuckle. LOVE holding the fork. HATE cutting into his steak.

My Father's Ghost,
My Father's Father's Ghost,
and the Wiles of Eternity

Little Cat's Feet

My father told me he could feel the ghost of *his* father in the house. And, occasionally, the ghost of a favorite uncle who kept a wad of cash in an old boxing glove. My father said the uncle came to haunt him, just a bit, knocking over stuff in the basement late at night. But that his dad would move on little cat's feet. Never seen of course, but you could feel him creeping around the place, my father said about his dad. As a kid I was always a little spooked. Hoping I wouldn't run into either of them.

Now that my father has passed, I don't hear a thing from him. Just sense the occasional stir of air one might feel from a jogger running by now and then. Too subtle to count, when I want so much to want it to.

You Never Run Out of Plus Signs

My wife and I discuss eternity. "As far as I can fit it in my head to keep myself from getting a headache," she says, "is to think of it as an incredibly high number in time and you just keep adding plus signs. Like, you never run out of plus signs."

"I mean, how boring would that be?" I say. "Who would want that? To live for eternity in any form, in any context."

"You're giving me a headache," she says.

Green

My dad said he bought cigarettes (cartons) and got a cheap ring for a girlfriend with the money he stole from his Uncle's boxing glove. Said he was just trying to put it on when he discovered all that cash. How sorry he was his uncle died before he had a chance to pay him back. But that he'd meet that uncle in Heaven someday and apologize. The boxing glove, he said, was leather and cracked from age and use, but was plump with what mattered. When I asked how he managed to fill it with all that cash on a gravedigger's salary, he told me, "Never you mind." I try to imagine all the plus signs my father must have imagined. The endless apologies he'd have to make with all that time on their hands. How good those cigarettes must have tasted, and how green his girlfriend's finger must have been when she took that cheap ring off. How the ghost of it, when they split up, might have haunted her.

A Short History of Whispers, Ditties, and Tasty Ghost Parts

The Size and Shape of Whispers

Ray goes into the baby's room and gives his infant daughter a bottle. Once she is asleep he whispers into the two-way baby monitor. His wife on the other end, throws back the covers.

"This is Mr. Big," Ray says in a deep low voice. "I'm only in town for a day and I'm looking for action."

"Action's my middle name," Ursula says in a whisper.

"What's your first?"

"Petunia."

Ray stifles a laugh. "Well, Petunia, I'll be right over with bells on."

"No, no bells. You might wake the baby. Where are you?"

"Under a lamppost in the fog smoking a cigarette. A stinky French one."

"Mr. Big, huh," Ursula says. "They call you that because of your nose or you got so much freight you need a wheelbarrow to get around?"

Ray can no longer control it. He laughs. The baby wakes and cries. Ray hears his wife say: "Shit!" through the monitor in more than a whisper.

Ditty-Interruptus

When Ray was young his father was teaching him how to tie his shoes when his father fell over dead. There was a little instructive rhyme Ray's father was reciting. His father would bend down, grab the laces and say in singsong: "Criss-cross down, loop around, push through, pull down." This time he only got as far as "loop around" when he clutched his chest, made harsh gurgling sounds, then pitched forward onto the carpet.

Ray didn't know what to make of it. Was his father playacting like he often did? Or was this part of his shoelace-tying training, some playful addition. When his mother walked in and screamed, he knew bad things would follow.

That little ditty still haunts him somewhat. But it is just a small kick in the pants to the ghost of it once he gets past the "loop around" part as he teaches his daughter (five now) the instructive rhyme and makes it all the way to the end with his circulatory system at full function. They are in the bathroom when he notices his daughter's shoe is untied. His wife is in the shower singing. It's a song he never liked, yet somehow (between the acoustics and the moment) he finds it unaccountably appealing, especially when she hits the last high note.

Ghost Parts

Ray's father had one good eye, the other was made of glass. When his dad was a kid he tossed old 78 rpm opera records up into the air as his older brother fired at them with a shotgun. A snippet of an aria found its way into the younger brother's right eye, erasing the world from it forever.

Ray's father's fake eye was a work of art, matching the other eye eerily. It floated in his head like a dead fish, and when his father was cross, or even when he wasn't (looking up from a shoelace, say), Ray would stare at it, and only rarely into the one that took him in.

Ray and Ursula's daughter is all grown now (is a first-year medical student) and cooking them breakfast. She is making pancakes in the shape of different body parts. "Guess?" she says, proud of her tasty representations: a four-fingered hand, an eye, lips formed into a smile … Some are easily recognizable and others a bit more amoeboid as they spread in the pan. Ray and Ursula take turns naming them. Ray pours syrup over an anatomical heap. "Good," he says chewing on the fifth finger he's named and what looks like an ear (sort of) and what he'll find out later was a heart beside a pancreas … But cannot put a fork into that eye (easily discernable) peering, syrup-soaked, unblinking—helplessly gazing up at him.

Jesus in a Coffee Cup
(East Harlem, NY)

Vacuum Cleaner TV

I find it stunning how much of Jesus (halo included) can be stuffed inside my mother's small TV. All of Him, malleable enough to fit, seated beside all those holy rollers speaking for Him like ventriloquist's dummies. The reverentially shut eyes, the bowed heads, their two-syllable incantation: "Jeee-suss!"—over and over. Jesus' mouthpieces like giant vacuum cleaners sucking into the night. My mother donating the little she had, drawn into the set with all the rest of her.

Lincoln Without the Beard

My mother tells me she has an eye floater that looks a lot like Jimmy, this smarmy guy she was seeing after my father left. (In profile, she tells me.) He was a low-level runner for the mob. He had unbearably stinky feet and took his shoes off, first thing, and put them up imperially onto our coffee table.

My sister would nearly empty a can of hairspray as she entered the room, her hair so stiff you could snap off pieces of it. My mother kept finding ghost roaches to bug spray on the baseboard by the couch he sat on. Anything was better. I opened windows, even in winter.

When they broke up Jimmy threw the small TV he got us out the window into the backyard five floors below. There was an old Italian wino down there who sang for spare change that people tossed from their tenement windows. Mostly pennies. He stopped in the middle of *Male Femina* as heads flew out of windows cursing the interruption. Then it all started up again, the singing, like nothing happened. It was that kind of neighborhood.

On good days, my mother says, the floater looks like Lincoln without the beard (which I find hard to picture). "But unfortunately there are never enough good days," she tells me.

Visitation Rights

When I was fourteen my father wanted to get me free weights to fill the spaces between skin and bone, espousing the virtues of *heft*. I wanted a typewriter. I had little poems I needed to click out of me. He said, "How many times do you think you'd have to lift a typewriter to get the job done?"

My mother finds pareidolia in odd places: Jesus in the coffee creamer she refuses to stir, the Virgin Mary in the cat's rump fur when it lifts its tail. (A location I find "ungodly.") To me the latter looks more like an Eskimo wearing a hoodie. But I don't tell her that. My mother mixes cake batter. With all that chocolate in a swirl (and all that *need*) you just never know who might show up.

How Joey Z. Saved Us All
(East Harlem, NY)

Homemade

It was Joey taught us how to make a *zip gun*: car antenna for a
barrel, a piece of two-by-four: the frame. Some friction tape
to hold it all together. Rubber bands around a pointy nail to
detonate the round—a .22 and *Bam!*

It either put a hole in someone's head or blew up in your
face. "50/50," Joey said. "The odds. Not bad."

Snap, Crackle, and Pop

In a yard between the old tenements, Joey built a fire—held
out fat bullets stolen from his dad. Had us stand in a circle
around the flames as he tossed them in. When the first round
ricocheted against a wall, we scattered quick as sparrows,
turned only from a distance as one by one the bullets popped
and zinged—saw Joey, eyes shut, saying, "Shit! Holy shit!" His
feet rooted where we left them.

How Joey Saved Us

On a tenement rooftop, six stories higher than the street, than our stickball, our marbles, and our ease, Joey called us "girls" because no one volunteered to be the first to jump from roof to roof. Struck dumb among the pigeons on the sun-soft tar, we shrank beneath his disappointed gaze, as he stepped back, then back again, and took a running leap. Landed on the other side. Just. A crunch against the sliding gravel edge. The sudden stop angling him back. His arms windmilling hard to make up for it, but not enough to fight the pull. The only sound, the word: *"Damn!"* coming from his upside-down face—his arms still spinning, then the faraway, almost too soft thud of him landing.

My mother's words coming back to me: *"You need to stop hanging out with that kid!"*

So I did.

Randy

Randy

Grace screeched at the set when she saw her ex, Randy, in handcuffs with his head down, accused of being the "Pillow-case Killer!" How the hell could she not know? Picked up on it? Was her *Deadly Danger* detector switched off? Did she even have one? *My God!*

She remembered the few times she got him angry. How close? How friggin' close might she have come? How blind? How gullible? She recalled coming home with those beat-up shoes from the '30s that supposedly belonged to a great old blues singer, called "Blind Willie Jackson." The guy who sold them even had photos, said: "See," pointing to the singer's shoes. It was hard to tell. Shoes were shoes after all, but she'd always loved the blues and purchased them. That night when she showed them to Randy and told him what she paid, he shouted, "How fucking stupid can you be?" He clicked on the set (the news) and sat there smoldering. Was this before? Or— oh my god …

Randy

Moments came back to her, intrusively. She recalled one Halloween she and Randy carved a jack-o'-lantern together, put a small candle inside, and turned off all the lights. He, against her protestations, balanced the pumpkin on his head, precariously. The orange light had cast down a bit eerily upon his face, just enough to see that smile. "Ooooo," he said in a Halloweeny ghost voice and she quickly turned the lights back on. *Fuck!*

Randy

The victims were all found with pillowcases over their heads, it was determined, *prior* to strangulation. Randy was powerfully built, but had the weakest handshake a friend told her. What did he have to hide? Maybe everything? Was that a sign? Some "tell?" No, she couldn't believe that. She couldn't let that penetrate her brain, find an old couch to sit in there, take up residence. It had to be later. There were years after the break-up. There were years. *Her* Randy was not *that* Randy. He liked to snuggle and rub her shoulders … Shit!—shoulders were only inches from a throat—erase! Everyone loved Randy, except that one friend who said she couldn't trust a man with a handshake that weak. They watched fireflies at night. He was quick, she'd give him that. Plucked one right out of the air and squished it, turned it into a phosphorescent smear. That big hand he held up inches from her face, That smile. *Dear God!*

Death in the Afternoon

Cara

Cara finds the "tit pics" on her husband's phone. They are smaller, perkier than her own and she doesn't say a word about it to him. Just gives him the cold shoulder (which he brushes off like dandruff, clueless) and heads off to work.

When Cara picks their daughter, Sandy, up from school Sandy has two of her girlfriends with her who scurry into the back seat. A sleepover is planned. In no time the girls are all texting wildly into their phones. Cara cannot get the image of those nipples, and the direction they are pointing, out of her head as she enters the freeway with her hands too tightly on the wheel, a heavy foot on the gas. She hasn't smoked pot in years, but knows her teenage daughter does, regularly, because she's picked the lock to Sandy's diary. She even knows where her daughter keeps it. Decides it just might steady her nerves to have a few tokes.

"Okay," Cara says to the teenager beside her. "Fork it over." The two girls in the back look up.

Sandy turns. "What?"

"Gimme," her mother says with one hand on the wheel, the other extended. "Your father doesn't know. Let's keep it that way. But we'll talk about it later. And don't even think about denying it. It's in your make-up bag under all that crap. Now, missy."

"Mom!" The girl says.

"Now."

Sandy takes one of the three tightly rolled sticks of pot out and hands it over. The two girls in the back sit there with their mouths swung open as Cara pushes in the dash lighter and sets the tip on fire, inhales deeply.

Bob

Bob is on the freeway headed the other way. He's just gotten his pink slip after 21 years of working an assembly line. But between the arthritis in his hands and the pain killers he takes, he can no longer keep up, so now he is heading home to sulk with what's left of the bottle of E & J whiskey on his lap. The music (some hard rock station he never listens to) is turned up to distortion. "Fuck!—fuck!—fuck!" he says as he weaves from lane to lane, having a difficult time keeping within the dividing lines, his foot heavy on the gas. Bobbing his head unconsciously to a music he can't stand.

Cara and Bob

Cara has never smoked anything this strong. Sunlight strikes at her from car chrome and she squints, wishes she wasn't so distraught when she left and remembered to bring her sunglasses. "Wow," Cara says, "this shit is pow-er-ful,!" and the girls in the back giggle. But beside her, her daughter is knifing her with dirty looks. Finally, Sandy reaches over to take the joint from her mother's lips, when it tumbles from them and bounces off Cara's leg to the floor. Cara is, for a moment disoriented, looking down and around, hoping it hasn't landed in her lap. Cara's car is closest to the oncoming traffic that Bob is in, and she edges out of her lane and the girls scream as they see Bob's car get bigger and closer and the look on his drunken face in a flash. They are inches from collision when Cara spins the wheel with an adrenalin-rich response in time, keeping their various metals intact as she steadies the vehicle.

Bob lowers the radio and tosses the open bottle out the window. The girls in the back seat are holding each other's hands, squeezing, squeezing. Sandy finds what is left of the joint at her feet and presses it against the dash to put it out and returns it to her make-up bag, slaps her mother's arm hard, then cries.

Cara says, "Oh, honey ..." The wheel a part of her now, her eyes on the road. Bob eases his foot off the gas, marshals a reservoir of focus he keeps for such occasions, remains between the lane lines. Turns off the radio. Can hear a better music from a convertible that passes. The man driving it glances over and shakes his head.

Just off the freeway there is a stand of poplars and a field of wildflowers. High above it all is a hawk gliding with a descending corkscrew motion, circling lower and lower. It spots something with a keen eye cocked, and drops.

History Lesson

Audience

Pill bottles are on the nightstand like a medicine man's rattles laid down. Her granddaughter is on the edge of the bed, her smartphone is in her back pocket. There are no crazy-thumbs text ballets. This is live.

Beehives

"It was tough, our old neighborhood," Grandmother tells the girl. "Some of us had straight razors in our beehive hairdos. You wouldn't know nothin' about that. And those juke-boxes ..." The old woman strained a bit rising up on her pil-lows. "Those hunks they had back then singing in them juke-boxes all lit up. You wanted them to jump out and take you in their arms." A smile blossomed through the cracks. "And our lips were all lit up too—all those pretty colors—and every-body smoked then. There was an ashtray on every table in the diner where we hung out. All those painted filters in them sticking up. I wore the reddest lipstick. And one that was almost purple I wiped off before I went home. And the laughs. We were really somethin'. We gabbed a mile a minute. Dirty talk that made us choke sometimes on the smoke we laughed so hard. Stuff you have on TV nowadays like it's nothin', was really somethin' back then."

Snow Cave

"My dad drove a snowplow for the city. All the cars were covered over some winters and dark inside like caves. That snow really piled up. If my dad only knew …" The old woman paused to catch her breath. "We broke into one of them. A red Cadillac with leather seats. I remember how good they smelled. That's where your mom was made, surrounded by all that cold and all that heat." Her granddaughter squirmed a bit and hoped she hadn't butt-dialed anyone.

"He was a bad boy. One of the wild ones. But he lit my cigarette like a gentleman after, and went out first so he could open the door for me. You just don't see that anymore. I forget his name. It doesn't matter. Oh, honey, get me another one of those pills. No, the other bottle. The pretty blue ones and some water. My throat is dry from spillin' the beans. You wouldn't know nothin' about that neither. Probably don't have nothin' to spill yet. You keep it that way for as long as you can. There's no hurry, hon. Life will catch up on its own, no matter what. You'll see. It has a way of doing that."

Stuck

Through the Glass

I saw the conjoined twins staring through the window of the pet shop at the mall. Two young women fused together in what seemed a single body in a floral dress. One half of them laughed, waved an arm excitedly. But only one.

Through the Looking Glass

I'd come for a pair of dress trousers to wear to my daughter's graduation. Now I was struck by the things my daughter complained about: that tiny pimple which in her mind was lava-filled, volcanic, the grapes that were never sweet enough … I thought of my 23 years of marriage, how sometimes the house was never big enough. And those road trips: the straightjacket I needed to break out of, even if only for a moment alone, to gaze at a mountain or field of wildflowers at a rest stop.

Reflection

They were in the pet shop now. I edged toward the window. I tried to observe them without staring, but most likely did anyway. What if one of them met somebody, romantically? I thought. What level of illusion might it take for the other? What act of invisibility? What if one of them needed to take off running without the other? Or just sit in a room alone to think when the other wanted to sing or dance?

Inside the shop they were holding a kitten. I noticed how every eye was upon them. When I leaned closer to the glass, their heads rose, and for a horrible moment our collective eyes locked. (Pretend to be looking elsewhere, my mind said, to no abeyance). The kitten squirmed and they gazed down at it. It was as if some hot wire I clutched were suddenly unplugged, and I rushed away. Pushed into and against the gushing tide of shoppers feeling so alone, so alone, and simultaneously, so happy to be.

Slack Tide

Gunsight

She went out with a biker named Ned. He was in a motorcycle gang and said he snuck off to be with somebody with "kinder, softer sensibilities." That he craved it. Sometimes, though compelling, she found it hard to look at him. He had a tattoo around one eye which looked like the front end of a gun barrel with a sight and that eye of his at its center. Like she was looking down the barrel and that eye, with a charge of gunpowder behind it, was looking back at her. He wore snakeskin boots with embossed cobras coiled into the leather of each, that hung over the end of her bed when he stretched out.

She read him poetry (from a book he brought) as he rubbed her feet. He knew all the pressure points and body parts they corresponded to. Sometimes she'd stammer, or sigh, or shout out something which made no sense—abrupt and disjunctive—a Tourette's syndrome bounty of expletives spewed volcanically. Then she'd return to her soft-spoken recitation. He never said a word, just kept rubbing, finding all the right spots.

The Point in a Pencil Point

She took him to the pencil factory where her brother worked. Ned baked cookies the night before. She held a bag of them on her lap with one hand, the other snaked around his waist as the motorcycle raged. When her brother put a box of pencils on her lap in exchange for the cookies, he, though he tried not to, stared at that gun barrel eye as though he were making eye contact with a cyclops.

"Think of all the unexpressed words there are in those pencils, all pent up," Ned said, and her brother just kept gaping as if that one eyeball might shoot out and wound him.

"Fuckwad cattle piss!" his sister said, as they rumbled off.

Slack Tide

"Out there I feel like rough seas and loud waves crashing," he told her while he was mopping her kitchen floor. She stood in the doorway eating a carrot, hoping she wouldn't blurt out a fury of mangled swear words and choke to death.

"But here," he said with you, I feel more like a slack tide."

"What's that?" she said.

"That's when the water is calm."

"Cool," she said, "that you know that," thinking how small the mop looked. Then she said, "Hey, you big ox, you wanna fuck?"

He looked at her for a long moment, with two eyes and a gun barrel, then leaned the mop against the wall. He could feel the first waves of turbulence rising up inside him. Hoped it was just the Tourette's doing the talking.

The Pit

Big Red Crosses

Banks was with the prostitute in the back of the ambulance from another time/another war. It was 1967, and the ambulance was surplus from the '40s. It was green and decorated with giant red crosses. We were at the Tay Ninh dump, and the "lance" rocked a bit as I sat in the cab and smoked a joint, parked at the edge of the enormous pit.

Scrubbed

Inside the pit the mama-sans foraged through the rubble with kerchiefs over their faces like bandits. In time, old tires would become sandals, artillery shells converted into vases ornately etched with bucolic scenes from an idealized time: women with parasols under unblemished skies (scrubbed of war planes and helicopters), serene mountain backdrops. We'd dumped dozens of bags of blood atop the rubble. Blood that had gone bad. Sergeant Purcell stood at the edge of the pit and fired his M3 grease gun into it and laughed as the blood bags exploded into a generous spray onto everything nearby: a bloody Pollock painting from some unknown circle in Hell. Several mama-sans scattered up the sides of the great pit (or tried to) and the rats scurried deeper in, making the surface undulate.

The cab filled with smoke and I, with disgust. But Sergeant Purcell wanted his sense of humor to be a communicable disease, so when he turned and smiled, I gave him a thumbs up.

Black Cyclone

There was a small oblong window behind me and I turned to look inside. I could see only vague movements beyond a writhing black cyclone. The sound was familiar, a kind of whirring considerably muted by the cab wall between us. But that sound increased beyond any magnitude I could have imagined when the back doors blasted open all the way, and the prostitute and Banks darted out in a frenzy, slapping at themselves and waving away the storm of flies that encircled them in crazed tenacious orbits.

When I turned back, I could see Purcell point his gun at one of the mama-sans. She was trying to gain purchase up the edge of the pit, but in her panic, kept sliding back down. She was screaming and that made Purcell laugh even louder. There were several more bags of blood remaining not ruptured, and having had his fill of the hysterical old woman, he switched his focus and aimed at them. Eventually the flies would return to the pit, to that broader harvest, Banks and the Sergeant back to the lance, and there'd be another joint to pass.

There was a huge red cross on the roof of the lance, presumably to keep World War II aircraft from bombing and strafing them. The way I heard it, it was more a target than a deterrent. But that was another time, another story altogether.

Millie in Ascendance

From the Heavens

Millie was doing her nails in the parlor, when a part from a passing plane, crashed through the ceiling. Detaching like ordnance from a bomber. Altitude-frosted. Just missing her TV. Her favorite soap opera. The actors never missing a line, as Millie screamed and bolted from the house.

Mr. Bill

Millie, who worked the line at a frozen pizza plant, and was not acquainted with irony. Who never expected much out of life. Fame or fortune. Presented with the former, when the local media picked up the story and it went viral. Interviews on YouTube; telling how her Pomeranian, Mr. Bill, kept barking at it once he came out from behind the sofa.

Atomic

It was just another day, after all, and she had a new bottle of *Atomic Orange* nail polish she was trying out. And Bernice was breaking up with Howard on TV, and she never did get to see the look on his face when the *cheatin' son of a bitch got his*. But the airline was paying for the roof and rug, and then some. And ain't it funny how some things work out, not at all like you'd expect. And ain't it just crazy-mixed-up-really-something how it all can just turn around on a dime.

Evaporating Landscapes

9:32

I stand before you like a man straightening his toupee after an unexpected wind. Dignity after all. You, like a boxer on spaghetti legs. A night dropping down: a hat so large it covers our eyes completely. It is 9:32 in the morning.

At the Deep End of the Ocean Liner

We are waiting for *The Call*. A doctor who likes playing with his eyeglasses when he speaks behind a big desk. An ocean liner desk, with us on the other side, sinking.

The Call

The phone rings. We let it. Then put it on speaker. Hear the good news. The torpedoes whizzing by. The phone click. The long hug. A quick change into something more comfortable.

Sloppy and familiar. Something you swim in. Breaking the surface like a head through an old sweater. Sky and air and land, an inch away. The same terrain. The same terrain again. And, *Hey, what's for dinner?*

Horse's Ass

Inside

They are in the pantomime horse costume clomping comically about the lawn at their daughter's birthday party. She, at the front guiding them, and he, with his arms around her, the horse's disproportionally high rear. Occasionally she neighs and a few kids laugh. One girl pets its mane, then quickly scampers off.

"Neigh," she repeats into the din of squealing children.

"Giddy up," he tells her, gently tapping her rump. They are both sweating and the scent of her shampoo and perspiration arouses him.

"Quit it!" she says.

"Not so loud," he tells her.

"I saw the way you looked at Carmen earlier," she whispers. You really *are* a horse's ass."

"Carmen? She's old enough to be my grandmother."

"She's what, three years older than I am?"

"Well you look ten years younger."

"Ha! How does a horse's ass produce so much *bullshit?*"

"Good one," he says, "but it's for real, you know I only have eyes for you," and gives her another soft pat. Then he says, "Hey, let me know when you're going to make a sharp turn like that next time. You nearly split us in half."

Inside Out

They keep the horse costume. Occasionally they take it out of a dark corner of the closet and a good deal of creative foreplay ensues within its confines. They take turns regarding who will lead them to the bed and who will be the horse's ass. A great deal of contortionism is required and when they emerge, it is a kind of hatching: seeing each other anew.

Divided Up

He had, an hour earlier, made a musical instrument out of his lawn chair, using the spoon from his iced tea to tap out a Latin rhythm against the aluminum armrest. He quipped that he was serenading her, as she ate from a bag of doughnut holes, ignoring him.

He sits in it now reading *The Old Man and the Sea*. "Why would anyone want a big fish in the first place?" he says. "What's with Hemingway and Melville anyway?" he says. Then he flips the book over, butterflying against his thigh, gazes through a space between two hedges in their yard as Carmen dives into her pool next door. He feels a burning sensation (real or imagined) at the back of his neck. He turns.

"I have a superpower," she tells him.

"Oh?"

"Yes, I have x-ray intuition. I can see right through to the bone."

"That sounds painful," he says. She's wearing a favorite blouse he bought her in Mexico, with small mirrored pieces sewn into the front of it. He sees himself divided up as he gazes into them. A jet overhead scars its way through a clear blue patch. The burning sensation intensifies. He is relieved to look up, up, up at it, his whole head in the sky. Lost in its contrails.

Life-Forms

Multilingual

We're in the garden. There are fragrances there, fluent in many languages. Cassie digs, plants, pats the earth. We'll soon be wedding cake toppers—her lacy gown/my penguin-wear. There are wind chimes, tinkling. They were once blown into a tangle of silence. It took a while to untangle them. Perhaps there is a metaphor here. The story changes. We are continually winnowing it down (what is at stake) like Russian nesting dolls.

Her engagement ring is over an earth-crusted trowel, in league with sunlight. There will be a faint ghost of it on her finger when she takes it off at night. I'm in a lawn chair strumming a ukulele. She wants a baby. I want two dogs and a Harley. "No hurry," she tells me.

"People pray for a basketful and carry a cup," she told me once. You could break a tooth chewing on that one. As she goes back into the house, I glance at a rose she's brushed past, bobbing, then at the accordion folds of her shadow up the steps.

Bachelor Party

The stripper comes in with a behemoth in tow, slices through testosterone thick as whale blubber. She waves off light from her eyes. Someone gets a towel and puts it over the shade of a standing lamp. The dimmer light hides a bruise I noticed earlier, caked with make-up. Many of my friends are married. The "ball and chain" jokes morph into a sizzle with wide eyes on her: "Look-what-you'll-be-missing" eyes.

The behemoth speaks with a heavy Eastern European accent. He lays out some rules, then holds up a wall with his arms folded. A chair is placed in the center of the room and I'm in it. The striper unzips my trousers slowly like she is revealing the secrets of the universe. We waited this long, so what the hell? Then pant leg by pant leg she pulls off my jeans to cheers. I'm in my tighty-whities. My friends' expletives are small explosives with confetti inside. The behemoth has a boom box and plays some garment-shedding music she finds irresistible. She's pretty good. And fit. She's in no hurry. There is a restless shuffling from the watchers and I'm not certain, but I think I hear someone say, "Oh, momma!"

She's down to just her panties, turns her red-lacy butt to the revved up onlookers. Tony gets up and hollers something unintelligible, so exuberantly, he farts and everyone laughs. The behemoth does a "Sit the fuck down" gesture with his bearded head, and Tony does as he's told. She makes much of her lap-landing. Circles the runway, then gyrates down. The feverish hooting crescendos.

There is something overly floral about her. Not Cassie's garden. This is olfactory abuse. I feel her breath in my ear: "Now ain't you the show horse," she says. It sounds rehearsed. I smell something burning. It's not cigarette smoke or pot. "Shit," the behemoth says and turns like a weather vane and rushes to the lamp. The towel is nearly on fire.

"Do we really need protection?" Cassie says. "I mean, what are we actually protecting against? Let's roll the dice. Get frisky."

We are at a party. It's snowing out, lightly. Our coats are atop a pile on the bed, slightly damp, and Cassie finds the weighted sum of them inviting. She has stopped taking the pill, says they're making her moody. We're using condoms now. I haven't any. My brother is at the house feeding our two yellow labs. My Harley is in the garage waiting for spring. Waiting *to* spring. I want Cassie's arms around my waist and the world to whiz on by us, or seem to, as we whiz on by it. Velocity can air one out. Air two out in all the right ways.

Lately Cassie's been urging us to make love in odd places. Says she always wanted to make love in a barn, in a hammock, in a mall dressing room. Everyone is in the living room with their drinks and an ooze or riptide of gossip. We are in the bedroom of a close friend. Cassie is staring at the pile of coats and lifts one end. It is dark inside and there is the combined scents of all our friends (natural and unnatural) and a hint of the weather outside. When I was a kid my mother got me a book of snowflakes. A single flake for each slick page. I marveled at the sight of each in isolation. Nearly planetary. Each a unique, irreplicable art.

Currently they are merely damp spots on coats as Cassie smiles, goes to the door/the knob, and pushes in the lock button. Goes back and finds another cave entrance. I glance inside. "You've got to be kidding me," I say. There is no end in there, no top, no bottom—only future now.

Our Secrets Know the Scent of Us

The Edge

We are young, and the "stupid" gene is strong in us. There is
a cliff. Below is an ocean with raucous waves disassembling
against big rocks. There is 60 feet between us and all of that.
A few seagulls are screeching, gliding. Daring us, perhaps.
Young minds see danger through a haze, often reconfigured
into something else. There are three of us. I don't remember
who spotted the "something else" first. But the idea was to
cut up my T-shirt with Joey's penknife and make blindfolds.
We'd put them on and run toward the edge wrapped in all that
tarry darkness. See who stopped closest to the edge. They'd
be the winner. Would have the "biggest balls." (Big balls, like
shadows, can be larger than the objects that create them.)
Nothing matters more. Jonny says: "One, two, three—go!"
And in the blackened-out world I bolt, pierce through the *unseen*. Keep on when I want to stop. The seagulls vanish, there
is only my heartbeat everywhere! I keep going. Then I stop.
And now there is a new sound: screams. Not the gulls'. I rip
my blindfold off like a scab. I am a foot from the edge. When

I turn, they have their blindfolds under their chins. They are a great many paces behind me. "I was trying to stop you," Joey says. "Before you, you know … You crazy fuck!"

On the way home they pat me on the back. A lot. I watch their faces. There is something there that wasn't there before. Joey gives me his penknife. He tells me he wants me to have it. He takes off his shirt and gives me that too. It is a little big, but fits perfectly.

Our Secrets Know

I become a pilot, do aerobatic maneuvers at air shows: loops, rolls, spins, dives. I even close my eyes as I dive, open them just in time as the earth rushes up, pull out at the last minute to gasps from the crowd. But after a friend crashes into fiery bits, I learn the difference between quiet courage and reckless abandon. In time, I prefer the former. Fly a crop duster for a living. When I date online, I say I "skywrite." Find there is something unaccountably romantic about a plane's penmanship.

I meet Amelia on justfornow.com. We go up in a hot air balloon, sail over a cornfield I dusted with pesticides earlier that week.

"So lovely," she says, peering over the gondola. Then turns, asks if I have any secrets.

"Come again?" I say.

"Secrets are cagey little things. They know the scent of us," she says.

"The scent?"

"I'll start," she tells me. "I'll tell you one. I buy these paint-by-numbers boards. I've got stacks. You know, with those hokey scenes all divided into sections to fill in—all those numbers." We dip a bit too low and I make adjustments. There are phone poles with hot wires and treetops down there. I have my license, a good head on my shoulders, and yes, it is filled with secrets. Whose isn't?

I remembered how my father worked with metal and every kind of tool. And how he'd bend over those paint-by-numbers Christmas scenes and bright red barns on the weekends: a little brush in those calloused hands. How those hands would become genteel for a time, balletic within the margins. How my mother purged his paintings from the walls, and the garage became his gallery. How he'd pull his truck in and sit there sometimes and be somewhere/someone else.

"Well, I paint over them," she says, as if confessing to a murder. "Do my abstract painting over all that saccharine crap. Ironic, don't you think?" I nod. "I've even had shows," she says.

"Wow," I say.

"But no one knows what's underneath. That's my little secret. But now *you* know."

"Cool," I say.

"Your turn," she says.

"I fly a crop duster. We use pesticides," I say.

"Asshole!" she tells me.

Comfort Animals

I meet Jenny through: takingitslow.com. We click. She moves in after a time. We enjoy watching whodunit mystery shows. We're watching one on TV, waiting for the commercials to end. I think the sister, with the long fingernails she keeps clicking, did it. Jenny thinks the gardener, with the fake-looking handlebar mustache, did. My old frail cat, Lily, is on my head. She's been doing that for the past couple of days. Climbing up on the back of the couch, then partially onto my head, nesting there. I hardly move for fear she'll slip off.

I reach up gingerly and pet Lily—she purrs. We are each other's comfort animal. I ease her down, put her on my lap. Jenny rubs her ears. I can feel the lingering ghost-weight of her still up there. Jenny leans in. Our warmth combines.

Yet still, from time to time, there is a restless stir in me, and I dream about the gulls. Those noisy gulls everywhere, screeching. It's dark. It's always dark in those dreams because my eyes are shut, and I'm running. When I open them, there's only air beneath and all that light. And the gulls above, in all that sky.

How the Wind
Finds Solace Where it Can

Bloodline

Joel lives alone in a trailer park by a lake. He had a wife but now she lives three trailer parks over with a man, ten years her junior, with a plethora of angry animal tattoos. Joel watches now as a fat mosquito disrupts the air with its pestering drone, then rumbles past his ear with devilish amplification. It alights on his arm as he watches. He waits till it is fully inserted, then brings his hand down hard, smearing a streak of blood through a thicket of arm hairs. Wonders if there is some communion taking place, a commingling. Perhaps a nip earlier from that busty new gal who just moved in, or maybe one of the Garland sisters. Hell, maybe both sisters. He flicks the crumpled wreckage off, but leaves the blood trail, if only to imagine further where it might lead him.

Geometry Climbs Over

"I want to be like the wind," he tells her. "The way it has no need for geometry. No particular shape. Free, you know?"

She is painting her toenails. A different color for each. Her trailer is filled with her charcoal drawings. There is hardly enough room to get around. He is a big man, but remarkably light on his feet. "Nothing wrong with wanting to be unconventional," she says. She is using a TV guide to fan her toes. "I like that geometry thing," she says. "There's free spirit soaked all through it."

He clears his throat and puts his beer down. They look at each other.

"You thinking what I'm thinking?" she says. With all his geometry he gingerly tiptoes over several of her drawings to reach her.

Expansion is the Mother of Wind

In his constrictive box on wheels he explores alternatives for expansion, wears the Virtual Reality headset and is transported to a bubbly underworld. The day before he had an app that took him to the top of a New York City skyscraper under construction. Was a high steel worker inching his way across a girder like a tightrope walker. Now he is in watery depths. A stingray passes by his face and he gasps. He comes upon the deck of a sunken galleon. A great white grazes its broken mast. He feels unaccountably at home there. When he takes the headset off for a swallow of beer, he hears the neighbor's cat scratching at the door. There is yet interstellar exploration to be had, the view from Everest ... He lets the cat in and opens a can of tuna. "Make it snappy," he tells Sprinkles, sits at a little table, and lights up. Waits. There is a turtle ashtray with a concave shell he taps ash into. The trailer walls are a vise, but there is that little window across from him. There is a sky. There is a star-bright universe in the offing. There are planets. Asteroids. There is no less than the moon itself to walk on.

Acknowledgments

Grateful acknowledgement is made to the following publications in which these stories or earlier versions previously appeared:

"Niagara Falls" *Maryland Literary Review*
"Three Entries from a Somnambulist's Dictionary" *New World Writing*
"Birdcage" *Branching Out: International Tales of Brilliant Flash Fiction (anthology)*
"His Ink and Miss Atomic Bomb *The Journal of Compressed Creative Arts*
"Life-Forms" *Fractured Literature*
"Orange/Door Hinge" *Bending Genres Journal*
"Little Race Cars" *Fictive Dream*
"From a Hitman's Sketchy Last Will and Testament Written on a Placemat at The House of Pancakes" *Flash Boulevard*
"Disneyland on Mars" *25 Miles from Here (Pure Slush Anthology)*
"Squirm" *MacQueen's Quarterly; Best Small Fictions 2022*
"Chickens in the Parlor" *South Florida Poetry Journal; Best Microfiction 2022*
"Petrified" *Potato Soup Journal*
"Late Blooming Gigolo" *Flash: The Short-Short Story Magazine; Nothing Is Ever One Thing*
"Black Bananas" *Flash Boulevard*
"Headlines" *The Daily Drunk*
"A Sky Full of Crickets" *Heavy Feather Review*
"Brain Waves" *South Florida Poetry Journal*
"The Twins" *Growing Up—Lifespan Vol. 2 (Pure Slush Anthology)*
"How Joey Z. Saved Us All (East Harlem NY) *Storyscape; Measuring the Distance*

"Horse's Ass" *South Florida Poetry Journal*

"Millie in Ascendance" *What We Know So Far*

"Evaporating Landscapes" *Boston Literary Magazine; What We Know So Far (nominated for The Pushcart Prize)*

"The Small End of the Funnel" *Microfiction Monday; Microfiction Monday Anthology*

"The Widower's Feathers" *Everyone Quarterly*

"Rodeo Clown" *Pure Slush Anthology: Lifespan, "Work"* Volume #5

"From a Hitman's Sketchy Last Will and Testament Written on a Placemat at The House of Pancakes" *52/250 A Year of Flash Anthology*

"Petrified" *The Best of Potato Soup Journal 2021 Anthology*

About the Author

Robert Scotellaro's work has been included in W.W. Norton's *Flash Fiction International, Maryland Literary Review, Gargoyle, Matter Press, New World Writing, Best Small Fictions 2016, 2017*, and *2021, Best Microfiction 2020,* and elsewhere. He is the author of seven chapbooks, several books for children, and five flash fiction collections. He was the winner of *Zone 3's* Rainmaker Award in Poetry and the Blue Light Book Award for his fiction. His flash collection, *What Are the Chances?* (Press 53), was a finalist for the 2020 Big Other Book Award for fiction. A new chapbook of flash and micro stories, *God in a Can,* is scheduled for release in 2022 (Bamboo Dart Press). He has, along with James Thomas, co-edited *New Micro: Exceptionally Short Fiction,* published by W.W. Norton & Co. Robert is one of the founding donors to The Ransom Flash Fiction Collection at the University of Texas, Austin. He lives in San Francisco. Visit him at www.robertscotellaro.com.

Made in the USA
Columbia, SC
14 March 2022

57669763R00083